DISASTER STRIKES

OTHER BOOKS BY PENNY DRAPER

Terror at Turtle Mountain

Peril at Pier Nine

Graveyard of the Sea

A Terrible Roar of Water

Ice Storm

DAY OF THE CYCLONE

PENNY DRAPER

Edited by Barbara Sapergia
Cover and text design by Tania Craan
Typeset by Susan Buck
Printed and bound in Canada by Friesens

FSC
www.fsc.org
MIX
Paper from responsible sources
FSC® C016245

Library and Archives Canada Cataloguing in Publication

Draper, Penny, 1957-
Day of the cyclone / Penny Draper.
(Disaster strikes ; 7)
For ages 8-12.
ISBN 978-1-55050-478-1

1. Tornadoes--Saskatchewan--Regina--Juvenile fiction.
I. Title. II. Series: Draper, Penny, 1957- . Disaster strikes ; 7.

PS8607.R36D39 2012 jC813'.6 C2012-900427-8

Library of Congress Control Number 2012932999

2517 Victoria Avenue
Regina, Saskatchewan
Canada S4P 0T2
www.coteaubooks.com

Available in Canada from:
Publishers Group Canada
2440 Viking Way
Richmond, British Columbia
Canada V6V 1N2

Available in the US from:
Orca Book Publishers
www.orcabook.com
1-800-210-5277

10 9 8 7 6 5 4 3 2 1

Coteau Books gratefully acknowledges the financial support of its publishing program by: the Saskatchewan Arts Board, the Canada Council for the Arts, the Government of Canada through the Canada Book Fund, the Government of Saskatchewan through the Creative Economy Entrepreneurial Fund and the City of Regina Arts Commission.

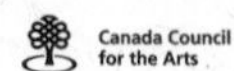

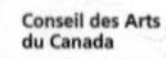

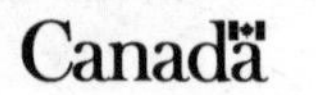

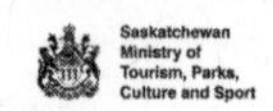

To Rush

TABLE OF CONTENTS

PROLOGUE

The Boy

Saskatchewan
Spring, 1912

The man reached out with a huge hand and grabbed his arm. "And where do you think you're going, boy?"

The boy struggled, partly in fear and partly in pain. The man was strong, and the boy was as skinny as a willow branch.

"Inside. Inside for dinner."

"Dinner?!" The man slapped him across the face. "You think you deserve dinner when your chores aren't done? Get on out to the yard – there's still wood to be chopped. Then maybe you can think about dinner. That is, if there's any left." The man chuckled at his own joke. There was never much left for the boy.

The man shoved him to the ground and added a kick or two for good measure. "Bloody orphans," he muttered as he walked away. "Bring 'em over from the old country to make my work easier and all I get is a snivelling weakling, moaning about how he's got to go to school. School?! When there's work to be done? Over my dead body."

The door to the tiny sod house slammed shut. As usual, the boy was left on the wrong side of it. His day had started hours and hours ago, before the sun was up. Now night had fallen and it was full dark. All he'd had to eat that day was some porridge and a bowl of boiled cabbage. He was exhausted, starving and angry. It wasn't fair.

Back in England, his mother had said it was like a dream come true. The famous Dr. Barnardo was taking orphans and boys from poor families and paying their passage to Canada to give them a fresh start and he – her very own boy – had been chosen. The doctor promised his mother that he'd be placed with a family; that he'd get to go to school.

"I feel like I'm cuttin' out me own heart, lettin' you go so far, but it's for the best," she'd said in her tearful goodbye. "You're the oldest, and you're the smartest. You deserve to make something of yourself and this be the only way. Work 'ard, and whatever else 'appens, go to school. If you get yourself educated, you can be a great man. A great man as can help 'is brothers what got left behind." Then she'd hugged him so tight he could barely breathe.

Canada. The reality was nothing like the dream. The boy picked up the axe and walked to the woodpile. He was so tired. His head hurt where the man had hit him. His empty belly cramped in pain.

The boy's face flushed in anger. He wasn't an orphan. He wasn't a weakling. And he would go to school.

The boy dropped the axe to the ground and walked out into the dark prairie night.

CHAPTER 1

Young Ladies Don't

Regina, 1912

"Don't fidget, dear," said Mrs. Barclay.

Ella made a face. "But this petticoat is so scratchy!" Mrs. Alexandra Barclay smiled fondly at her. Today was Ella's thirteenth birthday and her party guests were about to arrive. Her honey-coloured ringlets were curled into perfect sausages. She had a brand-new dress with a pale blue sash and a matching hair ribbon. Unfortunately the brand-new dress came with a petticoat underskirt made of miles of starched ruffles and bands of stiff horsehair.

"It is good practice to wear a petticoat, dear, remember that," replied her mother. "And the ruffles give your skirt such a pretty bounce. When you are older you will wear a corset as well as a petticoat."

Wonderful, thought Ella gloomily. She wished she were a boy. Not because she was a tomboy or anything, but it just seemed that the older she got the less she was allowed to do, at least if she wanted to be considered a proper young lady. Boys didn't have to look forward to corsets. Boys got to learn how to ride horses and work in a bank and go on trips and order other people around and the older they got, the more of it they got to do. Meanwhile, Ella and her friends had to stop running about, start wearing long skirts, learn all about housework, keep their eyes to the floor and practice perfect manners. Ella's life was becoming as scratchy as her petticoat. But there was no other choice, not when her mother was Mrs. Alexandra Barclay.

Mrs. Alexandra Barclay was considered a high society lady in Regina, and Regina was the capital of the entire province of Saskatchewan, so that made Mrs. Barclay especially important. She was thin and beautiful, her shiny blonde hair always twisted into a perfect chignon. She wore the right clothes, had impeccable manners and a rich husband to boot. But as far as Ella could tell, her mother didn't actually *do* anything. Except spend time making up rules for Ella to follow, of course.

Ella went back to squirming in her chair. Hands folded in the lap; look demurely at the floor; cross ankles but not legs. Ella was reminded every day by some rule or another that her parents were actually British, not Canadian. If they'd come from someplace else she was sure there wouldn't be so many silly rules. Regina was full of people who came from a million different places and Ella was certain none of them had to follow as many rules as she did. On top of that, her father, Mr. Leo Barclay, was the head of the biggest bank in Regina, so he was a very important man. Mother said it was important for his sake to "keep up appearances," which on her birthday apparently required a stupid, scratchy petticoat.

The doorbell rang. Finally! She jumped up from her chair

to run to the front door. Mrs. Barclay frowned, so Ella turned back and dutifully went to stand beside her at the door of the parlour while Mrs. Dudek, their housekeeper, answered the door. Rules, rules, rules. Could she ever remember all the things she was supposed to do?

All the girls from her class at school, along with their mothers, were invited to her party. Ella did her best to remember her manners. There were little sandwiches and cakes to eat, tea for the ladies and hot chocolate for the girls. When Ella was little, there used to be games too but Mrs. Barclay thought she was too old for games now. Luckily there were still presents.

Ella received four white handkerchiefs, one with her initial embroidered in the corner and three with tiny flowers. Useful. There was a "diary of feelings" – "You can write down everything that happens in your life!" gushed a girl Ella barely knew. Ugh. Last thing Ella wanted to do. Another book – that was hopeful. She unwrapped *The Empire Annual for Girls.*

"Lovely!" exclaimed Mrs. Barclay. "There are many good lessons to be had between those covers, Ella." Lessons? That sounded ominous. If her mother thought it was a good book, Ella was pretty sure she wouldn't. But she managed a thank you anyway.

There were two china teacups for her hope chest, and even one silver teaspoon from her mother. Ella thanked her politely.

"It takes time to build your hope chest," smiled her mother. "You're lucky to be starting so young." Inwardly Ella sighed. It was hard to get excited about china cups and silver spoons.

Mrs. Barclay raised her eyebrows at Ella. It was time for her speech. Standing up, Ella tried not to tug on the horrible petticoat and began.

"I want to thank you all very much for coming to my party...um, my birthday celebration. And thank you for the lovely gifts. I shall," Ella glanced over at the teacups, "I shall treasure them and think of you when I use them." Ella gulped. This was hard, even though she'd practiced. What came next? She looked in desperation at her mother. Ms. Barclay gave a small nod at the tea table.

"Oh yeah. Please help yourselves to more tea and cake." Mrs. Barclay tightened her lips. Some of her friends held their hands over their mouths to stifle their giggles. No matter, the speech was over.

Just then, there was a commotion at the door. They could hear Mrs. Dudek murmuring to someone and all eyes went to the door. In a rush of bluster two large men stepped through the door and filled the room. All the women looked politely at the floor. The girls, not as well trained, stared at the younger of the two. He was so handsome! The young man flashed a jaunty grin as he bowed to the ladies. The older man was tall with a prosperous belly to offset his small, balding head. He wore pinstriped trousers and a snowy white shirt under a brocade waistcoat and pinstriped jacket. The chain of a gold pocket watch crossed his barrel chest. Anybody could tell just by looking that this was a man of power.

"Why, Mr. Barclay!" exclaimed Mrs. Barclay. "What a surprise! And Mr. Isbister as well!"

"A little bird told me that today is a special day in the Barclay household, is it not?" asked Mr. Barclay, as he looked at his daughter.

Ella jumped up and threw her arms around her father. "I

can't believe you came to my party, Daddy!" Certainly all the guests looked surprised as well. Mr. Barclay was a very busy man.

"I can only stay long enough for you to open…" and with that Mr. Barclay reached into his business case, "this!" With a flourish he presented Ella with a square box, beautifully wrapped and tied with a bow.

Ella tore into the paper, even though she could see her mother frown at her haste. She didn't care – her father had come home for her party! She couldn't believe it. They hardly ever saw him because of all his business at the bank. He arranged loans for homesteaders to help them buy farming equipment. With immigrants pouring into Canada from all over Europe and the United States, business was booming.

Ella gasped. Inside the square box was a magic machine. She couldn't describe it any other way. Carefully she lifted it out for all to see. Her gasp was echoed by everyone in the room.

It was an Eastman Kodak Brownie camera. A camera! Ella couldn't believe it. It was going to be *so* much more fun than a teacup! The little Brownie was just her size. She looked up at her father with wide eyes, speechless.

"Remember it's not just for amusement, young lady," he admonished. "It's for educational purposes. There are lots of things you can learn about the world through the lens of a camera."

"Thank you, Daddy!" breathed Ella.

"The camera needs to be filled with film. Each film lets you take six pictures and then you have to take the film to the drugstore for developing. I've set up a small account for you at Mr. Duncan's pharmacy, Ella, but don't be foolish with it. Each film costs fifteen cents, so I will expect you to manage the account wisely."

The other mothers had overcome their shock at the wonderful gift and were nodding at Mr. Barclay's words of wisdom. Of course a banker would teach his daughter to be wise about money. Mrs. Barclay said nothing.

"Well then, my dear, enjoy your celebration and I will look forward to examining your photographs soon. Mr. Isbister and I are on our way to an important meeting and must be off to the bank now."

"If I may, sir?" Mr. Isbister stepped forward deferentially, nodding to Mr. Barclay. "Many happy returns of the day, my dear Miss Barclay," he went on, as he presented the birthday girl with a lovely bouquet of hothouse flowers he'd been hiding behind his back.

The girls sighed in delight. Jesper Isbister was the dreamiest fellow in all of Regina, and Ella actually got to live with him! His father back in England was a real live duke and had decided to send his son to Canada to learn all about banking with his old friend Mr. Barclay. Jesper was tall and had dark hair just a little too long and wavy to be proper. His fine clothes made him look like a prince. His warm brown eyes made a girl want to faint. At least that's what her classmates thought. Ella thought they were all nuts.

They had decided that Ella should marry Jesper and become the first Duchess of Regina. Ella always snorted with laughter whenever her friends talked such nonsense. "He's the third son," she'd say scornfully. "Only first sons get to be dukes! Third sons have to make money to add to the family fortunes. That's why he's here, sillies!"

To which her friends would reply, "And what's so bad about

being rich? Either way, you've got the best chance to catch him, Ella!" Sometimes Ella thought her mother was of the same opinion. She was always partnering them up. But Ella thought the whole idea was stupid. Jesper was more like an annoying older brother than a suitor. He teased her all the time. Who would want to marry *that?*

Mr. Isbister bowed low to Ella and when their faces were close he winked at her. He made Ella want to groan, but knew she couldn't and that was exactly why he did it. He was so cheeky! Jesper grinned at her, then composed his face before turning back to her father. Mr. Barclay smiled indulgently at his young apprentice, then patted Ella on the shoulder and bowed to the mothers. "Mrs. Barclay, ladies. Good day to you all." Ella looked longingly at the door. She'd have preferred going with them to work at the bank to making small talk at her party.

The instant the men were gone all the girls crowded around Ella. "How does it work?" "Take a picture of us!" "Can I hold it?" Ella dug deeper into the box and found the manual. She quickly leafed through it.

"The instructions are forty-four pages long!" exclaimed Ella. "I don't think I can take a picture right away, not if film costs fifteen cents."

"That's very wise, Ella," said her mother briskly, as she took the camera away from Ella. "I'll put it away for now."

Ella knew her mother was right, but as her guests went back to eating cake and sipping hot chocolate her eyes kept straying to the cabinet that hid her new Brownie. She wanted the party to be over. She wanted to read that manual.

Finally most of the goodies were gone, the mothers had run

out of polite chatter and the girls were tired. Ella did her best to remember her "saying goodbye" manners as she thanked everyone for coming. At last Ella and her mother were alone in the parlour. Ella didn't know what she wanted to do first – get out of her petticoat or study the manual. Comfort won out and she raced for her room, tearing at the ties of the awful garment as she went.

"Ella!" her mother called after her in horror. "Young ladies don't undress in the hallway!"

But Ella didn't listen to what young ladies don't do. She'd probably heard it a million times before anyway. She quickly put on her everyday skirt and breathed a great sigh of relief.

CHAPTER 2

The Brownie

It was hard, hiding from the man. Night after night the boy travelled west and the whispers followed, always the whispers about the anger of the man, about what the man was going to do when he found the boy. The boy knew he couldn't let the man find him.

Finally the lights of the Queen City sparkled in the distance. Regina. The boy knew cities. He could get lost in a city. He could get so lost the man would never find him. If only he weren't so hungry.

The boy stayed in the shadows. He listened. The whispers there told him about the Palace Livery Stable on Lorne Street. The hiring hall, it was called. Pay was a dollar and a half a day, if you got picked. A dollar and a half! When the boy got there, it was full of boisterous men, talking and joking. There were no other boys. Then the hall grew quiet. The farmers had arrived.

The farmers walked up and down the hall. They looked everybody over then tapped one – or two or three – of the big, burly men on the shoulder. They were the lucky ones, hired for a day's work. The boy stood as straight and tall as he could, and flexed his arm muscles to make them look strong. But nobody tapped his shoulder. It was all over in minutes. Half the men were gone. The rest, grumbling, went on their way.

No job, no dollar and a half. What was he going to do?

Then the boy felt a tap on his shoulder.

"The name's Jock," said an odd little man. "You look hungry."

Mrs. Dudek stayed late to tidy up after the party.

"No dinner tonight, please, Mrs. Dudek," said Mrs. Barclay. "Ella and I are full of sandwiches and Mr. Barclay won't be home until late. Make sure you take some cake home for your children." Mrs. Dudek was from Poland. Her husband and eldest son stayed all year at their homestead working to clear the land, while Mrs. Dudek lived in town with the younger children so she could earn money for the equipment her husband needed. Mrs. Dudek always looked tired.

"Thank you, thank you, missus," she said, and minutes later the front door shut behind her. Ella cuddled up in the big easy chair with her camera manual. Mrs. Barclay sat on a straight-backed chair with her embroidery.

"Mother, the instructions take a long time to read but it actually looks pretty easy to take a picture," said Ella.

"Hmmphh," replied her mother.

Ella looked up, startled. *Hmmphh?* Mrs. Alexandra Barclay never said *Hmmphh!* "What's wrong, Mother?"

Only silence came from the straight-backed chair.

"Mother?" asked Ella again.

Mrs. Barclay was tight-lipped. "It is never appropriate to contradict one's husband, but in the matter of your birthday present I do wish your father had consulted with me first."

"But Mother, it's a wonderful present!"

"The camera is indeed a wonderful invention. But Ella, it is hardly appropriate for a young lady. By nature, a photographer must be a busybody, poking the camera lens into the business of others, capturing moments of a personal nature and recording them for the world to see. A young lady should *never* be a busybody, Ella."

Ella frowned. "But Mother, you saw how excited my classmates were! They all *wanted* me to take their picture."

"Of course they did. When someone takes a photograph, a person wants to look their best and today all the girls were dressed in their party clothes. But would they be so keen on a photograph if they had just fallen off a buggy and landed in the mud? Of course not. No one wants those moments captured forever. Promise me, Ella, that you will use your common sense and concentrate on pictures of..." Mrs. Barclay thought for a moment. "Sunsets. Horses. Flowers, perhaps."

That didn't sound very exciting.

They both went back to their work. Finally Ella finished reading all forty-four pages of the manual. She looked up and for a few moments watched her mother take tiny neat stitches in the pillowcase she was embroidering. Sewing intricate flowers on something nobody ever saw was SO dull. How could she stand it, night after night?

"Mother," asked Ella curiously, "did you ever want to have a job? A real job, I mean. A job of your own. Instead of being stuck in the house all the time?"

Mrs. Barclay looked quizzically at her daughter. "What kind of job?"

"A photographer, maybe? Or a teacher or a nurse? Maybe you could work in the bank with Daddy? I don't know, just *something*."

Her mother laughed. " But I *am* doing something, Ella. There is no greater joy than to smoothly manage a household and family for one's husband. You'll understand when you're older. And besides, I'm not 'in the house' all the time. I'm a very busy woman." Mrs. Barclay went back to her tiny, perfect stitches.

How could her mother stand such a boring life? There were a million things Ella wanted to do and embroidery wasn't one of them. She looked at her camera and smiled. It was her ticket out of the parlour.

The next day was Saturday. Ella decided to take her Brownie out for a walk. Dressed in a neat blue skirt, a shirtwaist blouse, a clean white pinafore and button-down shoes, she walked out into the tree-lined streets of the city. She tried to look about with a photographer's eye.

Finding a good shot wasn't easy. She shivered whenever she thought of the word "shot." The manual said the pictures that came from the Brownie were called "snapshots" or "shots." It seemed a very odd word to use – Ella didn't want to "shoot" anyone – but it was meant to mean "easy." The word was actually invented by real hunters. The manual said that a long time ago hunters used the word "snapshot" when they had to make a really quick shot, a shot so fast they didn't even have time to raise their guns to their shoulders and had to shoot from the hip. The Brownie worked the same way. Ella held tight to the little box camera as she walked.

Downtown Regina, where Ella lived, was a beautiful place.

Her street, Victoria Avenue, was full of grand three-storey homes made of red brick. Most had a big front porch for enjoying the cool breezes of the evening, and some had second-floor balconies as well. There were large bay windows with stained glass in them; there were even sidewalks and curbs on the big, wide streets. Regina was growing so fast that the houses were taller than the trees planted along the avenue, but the trees would grow. Right now, Regina's mayor was mostly concerned with building homes for all the people who wanted to come. More than a thousand people arrived in Canada every day hoping to make a new life, and Mayor McAra wanted to make sure a lot of them came to Regina. And now that Regina was the capital of Saskatchewan, even the government was getting a huge new house, called the Legislative Building, down at the lake. Everything in Regina was brand new.

Ella lived right down the street from Victoria Park. The park was sort of green and had a fountain in the middle. "Sort of green" because it was only five years old and the trees hadn't had much time to grow. On the other side of the park stood a big stone church and the new Carnegie Library. Ella loved the library. Her father's bank faced the park as well. She stooped to pat a little white dog and it tried to lick her face, making Ella laugh. The man walking the dog gave her a grin.

Ella had an idea. "May I take a picture of your dog?" she asked the man.

"Don't know if he'll sit still for you, but go ahead and try," he said in a friendly voice. Ella stooped down. Every time she got close enough to take the picture the dog jumped on her, wanting to play. She stood up and tried shooting from the hip like the manual said. Better, but that dog was like a bouncy ball. Finally he was still, for a second anyway, and Ella pushed the button. She heard a satisfying click. "I got it!" she said happily.

The man and the dog continued on their walk. Photography was harder than she'd thought. Maybe it would be better to learn on something that stayed still. She looked around the Park. Buildings didn't move. Ella snapped a picture of the Carnegie Library, the Methodist Church and Mr. Barclay's bank. She shot a picture of all the lovely homes on Smith Street. To please her mother, she took a picture of a beautiful red rose. Then she was done. A whole film gone, and only ten minutes had passed!

Ella decided to walk downtown to Mr. Duncan's pharmacy and hand the film in to be processed. Mr. Duncan showed Ella the special developing machine he had on loan from the Eastman Kodak company to process the pictures. "Come back this afternoon, Ella," he said. "I'll have the photos ready for you by then."

Ella could hardly wait. She felt as jumpy as the little white dog. But finally afternoon came and she went to collect her snapshots. She rushed home, clutching the envelope. Her father was in his study.

Ella knocked on the door. "Daddy, I have my first photographs," she called through the door. "Would you like to see them?" Mr. Barclay invited her in, and Ella laid the snapshots across his desk. They both looked at them closely.

"What's that?" asked Ella, pointed to a picture that was nothing but a blur.

"Hard to tell, isn't it?" laughed Mr. Barclay. "Did you try to shoot something that was moving?"

It was the little white dog. Ella was disappointed. "It's very difficult to get a good shot of anything in motion," said her father kindly. "These other photos are very good."

The picture of the Metropolitan Methodist Church had turned out well. It was kind of amazing, really, to see a great big building reproduced exactly on a tiny scrap of paper.

"That picture is kind of boring," said Ella, pointing at the picture she'd taken of Smith Street.

"Perhaps it's not the most exciting photo," agreed her father, "but it's very good just the same. I like the way you angled the camera so you could see both sides of the street. That's called 'perspective' and some photographers take a long time to learn how to capture it. Well done, Ella." Ella's eyes lit up at his praise. "And look what you can see at the end of the street. It's our new Legislative Building!" Mr. Barclay clearly had a good eye for photography. Ella hadn't even noticed the new building in the picture.

"I don't like that one," said Ella, pointing at the rose. "The colour is so beautiful in real life. The photo makes it look dead."

"Well, that's the trouble with black-and-white film. It's probably best to choose shots that are interesting for something other than colour, since the colour will disappear."

"So, no colour and no movement. So much for Mother's sunsets, flowers and horses," Ella grumbled. "What *should* I shoot?"

Mr. Barclay thought about it for a minute. "Photograph the thing that is unusual – the thing that doesn't fit with the rest of the scene. Ella, get your hat. We're going out." Ella's eyes widened in excitement. An outing with her father!

In no time, they were walking towards downtown. Mr. Barclay stopped.

"Ella, look around. What do you see?"

They both looked. Across the road was the Post Office, the Bank of Commerce, and sandwiched between them, the ramshackle Royal Restaurant.

"What doesn't belong?" asked Mr. Barclay.

"That's easy," replied Ella. "The Royal. The Post Office and the Bank are grand buildings made of stone. The Royal, well, Mother won't let me go in there!"

"And quite right she is," agreed Mr. Barclay. "What else do you see?"

Ella looked carefully. There were people going into the Post Office carrying letters. A man dressed very much like her father went into the bank. And standing in the alley between the Royal and the Bank was a real live Chinese man.

"Ella, if you took a picture of the Post Office or the Bank it would be very pretty, just like your picture of the Carnegie Library. But if you took a picture of all three buildings together, including the Royal and the Chinese man, the picture isn't just pretty, it's interesting. It asks a question. What made that man decide to live in a place so different from his own home?"

Ella looked harder. She saw it, she really did. "Now the picture tells a story!" she exclaimed.

"Exactly," said Mr. Barclay with satisfaction. "Find the story."

CHAPTER 3

Billy

The man and the boy huddled together in a small house by the railroad tracks. The boy was thoughtful. "Tell me again about the buffalo."

"Och, what a lad for stories! Verra well, here it be. Back before the white man did come, the first people lived off the herds of buffalo that walked the length o' the prairie as far as the eye could see. They used every part of the animals they killed, 'cept the bones. Them they stacked into huge heaps taller'n meself and wider than aboot five wagons all together. Piles and piles of bones. They thought that if they kept the bones the buffalo would come back to visit their dead ancestors. An' it worked. Every year the buffalo came. The people nivver went withoot."

Their single candle flickered. "Tell me again," asked the boy. "Tell me again what it was like to have your own land."

"Terrifying," chuckled the odd little man. "I don't mourn the loss of it, laddie. Workin' the land was like pourin' water into a pail with a hole in it. Always the feelin' that ye'd never be done, that the land was bigger and stronger than you was and the prairie wind would suck you dry while you be trying." The man looked around the tiny room and chuckled again. "This place is more me size. Safer.

"The prairie's like a woman, laddie, and don't ye forget it. Strong and fierce *and beautiful. Excitin' ta visit, but hard ta live with. Now I once knew a girl back in Glasgow just like that...but a wee laddie such as yourself be too young for that story!"*

The boy grinned. "Don't you worry, old man, I'm not so young. And I'm old enough to know this – I'm goin' to have a piece of this place. I'm tired of living between four walls. I done it all my life. I want more. And like me mam said, the first step is goin' to school."

"Away ye daftie! Ye won't get away with it, boy. Come out from hidin' and they'll find ye," said the man. "They'll send ye back."

"Not if I'm smart," replied the boy. "I kin make up a story and get 'em all to believe me. Listen, I'm going to the Palace Livery. There's an immigrant train due from America. Those farmers are rich; they've got lots of gear. I can maybe make a dollar or two feeding their animals once they get off the train. Then I'll buy us some meal tickets, all right?"

"Ah couldna agree more," said the old man. "Git us a wee bit o' that good Chinese grub, will ye?"

On Monday, Ella decided to take her Brownie to school. The moment she arrived on the playground her friends crowded around. "Do you know how to take a picture yet?" "Take me, take me!" "Look at Ella's Brownie!" There was such a commotion that their teacher, Miss Hayward, came out to see what was going on.

"A Brownie! How very lucky you are, Ella," she exclaimed. "Perhaps you would like to take a photograph of your class?" There were shrieks of delight from the other students. "Yes, Ella, please do!"

Ella was nervous. Her classmates pushed and shoved for the best spots as Miss Hayward tried to get them into neat rows.

Ella held the camera at her waist and looked down into the viewfinder. Her jostling classmates had magically appeared inside the box, the size of tiny ants. "Hold still," she called out. Ella held her breath, just like the manual said. If you held your breath, the camera wouldn't jiggle. She didn't want another blurry snapshot. "Ready – one, two, three!" She pushed the button, and they all heard a click.

"When can we see it?" they all demanded, crowding around. "How do you get it out of the box?" Ella tried to answer their questions, and gradually her classmates lost interest and went back to playing. Ella slowly let her breath out. Taking pictures was hard work! She hoped the photograph would turn out. As she waited for the bell to ring, she looked around for other shots and that's when she saw the boy.

It was her father's words that made her notice him. *Look for the story.* For sure, this boy didn't belong at her school. She'd never seen him before. He was very thin, too thin, but had huge muscles as if he were really strong. And his clothes didn't fit. The trousers were too short for his long legs, and too wide. He was using an old piece of rope tied as a belt to hold them up. His workboots had holes in the leather soles and he had no socks. He was standing apart from all the other boys, who were clearly trying hard to ignore the strange newcomer. Ella couldn't tell if the boy looked fierce, or scared. A little of both, maybe. She looked at her camera. It was a good shot. It was a story.

Don't be a busybody. Her mother's words niggled at her brain. A real photographer surely didn't worry about being a busybody. Ella pushed the button. At the sound of the loud click the boy looked straight at her. Now Ella was sure. He looked fierce.

The boy came straight for her. He grabbed the Brownie right out of her hands.

"Who said you could take me picture?" he demanded. "What are you goin' to do with it?"

He talked funny. Kind of like Mr. Isbister, but not. Not high class, more like maybe he wasn't very smart. Ella shook her head. Why did she even care how he talked, when it looked like he was about to hit her? Ella took a step back and swallowed hard.

"I'm sorry," she stammered. "None of the other kids minded, so I didn't think you would either."

"Why do you want me picture?" the boy repeated angrily.

"I thought you looked...interesting," Ella squeaked out.

"Interestin,'" snorted the boy. "I'm real interestin,' all right." He strode away.

"Hey!" she shouted, running after him. "Give it back! That's mine!"

The boy looked at the Brownie as if he'd forgotten he even had it. "'ere, catch!" he said, as he threw it high in the air.

Her camera! Ella dashed forward, tripped, and fell to her knees in the schoolyard. The boy leapt lightly and caught the camera himself. Quick as lightning, he aimed the Brownie at Ella and she heard a click.

"See 'ow you like it!" he smirked.

Ella was frozen. Still on her hands and knees, she hung her head so that her ringlets would hide the furious tears rolling down her cheeks. She had never been so humiliated. And her knees hurt. And he still had her Brownie. And there was a picture of her inside it. And she hated whoever he was forever and ever.

There was absolute silence in the schoolyard. Every student stopped to stare. No one knew what to do. It was like both Ella and the boy were silently shouting "Don't touch me!" to everyone.

Into the silence came the jarring sound of the school bell. It broke the spell. The girls ran to Ella and helped her up. Ella used one of her new handkerchiefs to dab at the blood on her scraped knees. She tried not to let anyone see her tears. The rest of the students filed into the school. Some of the bigger boys bumped and shoved the new kid accidentally on purpose as they went by. One of them, Douglas Hindson, grabbed Ella's Brownie out of the boy's hand and brought it back to her. She smiled at Douglas. He was fifteen and his smile did more for Ella than Jesper's ever had. Ella took back her camera and walked into the school with Douglas. That almost made the incident worthwhile, thought Ella. She barely felt her scraped knees.

Soon the only student left in the schoolyard was the boy.

Ella glanced behind her for a moment. The boy turned, as if to leave. Then, with a sigh, he turned back and followed the others into class.

"Class, I would like to introduce Billy Forsythe, a new student," said Miss Hayward with a smile. The new boy stood uneasily beside her at the front of the room. "He has come all the way from London, England, to visit with his uncle, Mr. Leatherby of Lorne Street, whom I'm sure you all know."

Well, not exactly, thought Ella. Mr. Leatherby was a hermit. Everybody knew *of* him, but nobody really *knew* him. He lived in a big old house with a tower that they all called the Turret

House. He never came out and nobody ever went in. Deliveries were left on the back porch. He paid his bills, so it was assumed the old man was still alive, but his beautiful house was falling apart around him for lack of care. Maybe this Billy Forsythe was supposed to look after him or something. That was clearly a poor idea, thought Ella angrily. The boy was a monster. Maybe he'd kill Mr. Leatherby in his sleep.

"Please welcome Billy to our class." There was silence. "Class!" exclaimed Miss Hayward as she rapped her desk with a ruler. "Manners!"

A few mumbled hellos could be heard. Miss Hayward frowned. "Well," she said, turning to Billy, "I'm sure you will make friends very soon. Please sit at the empty desk over there." The empty desk was right beside Ella. She glared at Billy as he sat down. She wouldn't be his friend, that was for sure.

Ella studiously ignored Billy as they sang "God Save the King" and said the Lord's Prayer. When Miss Hayward turned her back to write the arithmetic questions on the blackboard, Billy grabbed Ella's arm.

"Listen, I didn't mean ta make you fall. I'm that sorry."

Ella pulled her arm away. "Don't touch me!" The boy shrank back into his seat.

Never had she worked so diligently on her long division. And as usual, working with numbers calmed her. Numbers had an orderliness that Ella truly enjoyed, even though she pretended to hate math just as much as all her friends. She was her father's daughter, after all. *There,* she thought. *Remainder equals two.* She was done. With a flourish she signed her name to her paper and stood to take it to Miss Hayward.

As she came back to her desk, she couldn't help but see Billy, head down over a rough sheet of paper that looked like it had been torn out of another book. He looked utterly confused. *Hmmphh,* sniffed Ella, in imitation of her mother. *He can't even do the work.*

At lunch, Billy sat alone, hands in his lap. Ella and her friends sat as far away from him as possible as they opened their lunch pails and shared their food. "That was so mean!" said one girl. "Throwing your Brownie like that. It could've broken!"

"Why do you think he's going to live with Mr. Leatherby?" asked another. "He's too young to look after the old man if he's sick."

"Maybe he doesn't want to look after him. Maybe he wants to help him die real fast so he can take all Mr. Leatherby's money!" the first girl said.

"That's an awful thing to say!"

"I don't think he's smart enough to figure out a scheme like that," said Ella unkindly. "He couldn't even do the long division problems this morning."

"Does Mr. Leatherby even have any money?" asked the second girl. "My mother said a strong wind would blow that house over, it's in such bad shape."

"I bet he's a miser and has pots and pots of gold in his basement!" replied the first girl. "Just like in books!"

Ella wasn't listening any more. She wasn't much interested in Mr. Leatherby. She was watching Billy. The older boys were walking over to him. Douglas was carrying a ball. Ella couldn't hear what Douglas said, but she could see Billy's eyes light up as he stood and joined the group. The boys all spread out in a circle around Billy. The boy with the ball threw it across the circle and a game of dodge ball was on.

Billy was fast, Ella had to give him that. He dodged the first ball with ease. And the second, and the third. He leapt, he ducked, he dove. All those muscles were good for something, even if he was ridiculously skinny. But then more balls appeared. They started flying from every point on the circle. Billy's head was swivelling like a top, trying to see all the missiles. He spun around and around but there were too many balls. Ella could see that Billy was starting to tire and as she watched, one of the balls hit him hard on the shin. He was out. But before he could leave the circle, he had to dodge another ball, and another and another. The boys just wouldn't stop. Billy was hit on the shoulder, on the arm, even on his head. He tried to catch the balls to stop the pummelling but there were too many flying at him.

He was being punished. Because of what he'd done to her.

Ella felt a warm little glow around her heart. She hadn't known the older boys even noticed her, let alone that they'd be willing to defend her against an outsider. But that's just what they were doing. As Ella watched, a ball came flying out of nowhere and hit Billy square on the back. He went down on his hands and knees.

Billy leapt to his feet and rushed towards the boy who had thrown the last ball. The fight was on. It was no contest right from the start. Billy was only half the size of the other boy but clearly knew how to fight. One punch to the jaw and the big boy was down with Billy on top of him. The two of them wrestled in the dust but Billy was always on top. Ella had never seen a real fight before. She knew there were fights in the Warehouse District on Saturday nights, but that was a rough neighbourhood where the men drank too much liquor. The kind of people Ella and her family knew would *never* fight. Without even thinking about it, Ella raised her Brownie and snapped a picture.

When it was clear that Billy wouldn't stop until he was forced, Douglas pulled him off the dodge ball player. As the players helped up their friend, Billy stood and watched. Then he turned on his heel and left the schoolyard. He didn't come back to class that afternoon.

Good riddance, thought Ella.

After school, all the girls who lived near Ella left the schoolyard together. All anyone could talk about was the fight. It was making Ella feel uncomfortable, since she seemed to be in the centre of the mess. With some relief, she turned down Scarth Street and waved goodbye to the other girls. But she didn't go home. She couldn't go home. Her stockings were torn and her knees were starting to scab over. Her mother would know something was wrong, she always knew. *Don't be a busybody.* She would be in so much trouble. Not even her father would forgive her this, if he found out. Being the cause of a fight was too far outside the rules even for him. And what about the pictures? Inside the camera was one of the boy, one of her on her knees, and one of the fight. They were proof she'd done exactly what her mother had told her not to do. How was she ever going to be able to explain them? She'd found a story all right, but not one she could tell.

Ella sat on a bench in Victoria Park, watching the fountain. She snapped another photo of it. That, at least, was one she could show her father, even if it wasn't interesting, even if it didn't tell a story. It was safe.

" 'ello?" came a voice from behind her.

Ella stood up in a rush. She clenched her fists and slowly turned around to look at Billy.

"Go away," she said fiercely.

"No."

"How dare you!"

"How dare I what?" Billy asked mildly. "I ain't doin' anyfing to you."

"You're making me angry, that's what!"

The boy had the gall to grin at her. "How'm I doin' that? I'm just standin' 'ere."

Ella wanted to scream. "You made me look like a fool, down on my hands and knees. You started a fight which was NOT my fault. You ruined my stockings and wasted a picture." Ella started to run out of steam. "Your very existence makes me angry! Isn't that ENOUGH?"

Billy laughed right out loud. "Talk about gettin' your knickers in a twist! Your own existence can't be very excitin' if what 'appened at school today is big news."

"You," Ella pointed her finger at him, "you know nothing. I don't know where you come from but getting into fights is not how we behave here. So for your information, *it is big news.*"

"Whoa. Excuse me. Where I come from that sorta fing means nuthin.' Me'n me bruvvers fight like that all the time. It just comes natural."

"Your brothers?" asked Ella.

"They ain't 'ere, they's back with me mam," replied Billy.

"In England?"

Billy nodded.

"So what are *you* doing here? In Regina, I mean. You haven't exactly made a good start at school, you know," said Ella in a bossy sort of voice.

"Not exactly me fault, now is it?" retorted Billy. "You went and started it."

"I wasn't the one who got in a fight, now was I?" she shot back.

Billy looked at her knees. "I dunno," he said with a smile. "Kinda looks like you was."

Ella looked down at her knees, then frowned at Billy. "My mother's going to kill me. Young ladies absolutely are not allowed to have scabby knees, no matter how they got them."

"Sneak in, then mend the 'oles afore she sees," advised Billy.

"I'm not very good at darning yet," sighed Ella. "It's so boring."

"Ach, it ain't 'ard," replied Billy.

"YOU know how to darn stockings?" asked Ella in disbelief.

"Course. You gotta, if you've got only one pair of socks."

Ella looked pointedly at Billy's feet. "Doesn't look like you've got any. And you don't look like the nephew of Mr. Leatherby, who would most certainly own at least three pairs of socks. Are you really living there? Nobody believes that, you know, not looking as you do."

"Too bad for them," retorted Billy. " 'Cause I do. So I'm the poor relation, okay? And Mr. Leatherby ain't one for buying extra pairs of socks. He'll come 'round, you'll see."

"Well," said Ella dubiously, "Try for a pair of trousers that fit too. Surely he can spring for those as well." She sighed. "I really want to hate you."

"Why?" asked Billy curiously. "It's too bad you fell, but everybody falls – who cares? And you can throw the picture away."

"Those pictures cost money, you know," said Ella ruefully. "And that one is wasted. No, it's because you made me feel bad. You were right and I was wrong. I shouldn't have taken your picture without asking. And then all that other bad stuff happened because of it."

A dark cloud passed over Billy's eyes. "Yeah, well bad stuff 'appens, whether it should or not. I only came over 'ere to say I's sorry," he said quietly. "You just surprised me and I don't really like people takin' my picture, you know, and I meant nothin' by throwing your camera in the air." The words all came out in such a rush Ella could barely understand him. He stuck out his hand.

"Hello, Ella whatever-fancy-last-name-you-have. I am Billy Forsythe and I would like to start again."

For some reason, the request delighted Ella. She forgot she'd promised never to be his friend. Billy's smile was even broader and brighter than Douglas's. Billy was interesting, he was different, and he tasted of adventure. Her mother would have a fit. No matter. Choosing her friends was up to her, not her mother.

Ella shook Billy's hand.

CHAPTER 4

The Work Party

It was full dark. The boy crept down the alley behind the store. When he got to the back door, he looked all around. There was nobody watching. Reaching into his boot, he pulled out his slim knife and slipped it into the keyhole. He worked the knife this way and that until he heard a click. It sounded so loud in the darkness. The boy froze and remained motionless, trying to blend into the darkness. Then he slowly looked about – still nobody around. Hoping the door didn't squeak, he carefully cracked it open just enough for his thin body to slip through. He was in.

The job wasn't going to be easy. It wasn't as if he was used to shopping in grand stores such as this. As quiet as a mouse, the boy went up and down the aisles until he saw a sign. With difficulty he sounded out the letters. B-O-Y-S C-L-O-T-H-E-S. It was the right place. He chose two shirts, a pair of trousers and a pair of socks. He looked longingly at the new boots, but he knew he'd never be able to afford them. He bundled up the clothing then headed to the stationery section. There he chose a brand-new notebook and two pencils. He was all set.

Squatting down in the aisle, right then and there, the boy took one of the pencils and opened the notebook. The first page was so clean and white! He was afraid to mess it up. But he had to. Carefully, in a scrawling hand, the boy wrote:

one trowsers – $2.00

one sok – 15 cents

2 shirt – 65 cents each

1 book – 10 cents

2 pensils – 5 cents

I.O.U.

He'd pay the store back. Some day. Then as quietly as he had arrived, he was gone into the night.

"Ella, dear," I would like you to accompany me," said Mrs. Barclay firmly at breakfast.

Ella didn't dare groan out loud, but she groaned plenty loud inside her head. It was Saturday! She wanted to take her Brownie down to Wascana Lake to find some interesting stories. The last thing on her list of fun things to do was to attend one of her mother's "Ladies" meetings.

"Do I have to wear my new petticoat?" asked Ella glumly. Mrs. Barclay allowed herself a small smile.

"No, Ella. This is a work party."

Work? What kind of work did the ladies do? More embroidery? There had to be something more interesting to do than chitchat with other women about how to get the laundry white and the banisters shiny and dinner on the table at exactly six o'clock. And how to make sure your daughters grew up just like you. Ella was determined not to let that happen. But sometimes it felt like she was going to have to break out of jail to escape it.

Jesper Isbister was taking breakfast with them. "My dear

Mrs. Barclay," he said. "May I escort you two lovely ladies to your engagement this morning?"

"You are always the perfect gentleman," smiled Mrs. Barclay. "That would be lovely. We leave at ten o'clock. Eat your breakfast, Ella. Don't be late." With that, her mother swept regally out of the room.

"And is the lovely Ella looking forward to a fun-filled Saturday?" teased Jesper. "Planning good works with your mother?"

"Don't make it worse, Jesper," she said gloomily.

"No more Mr. Isbister? Oh, I'm hurt!" Jesper exclaimed theatrically.

"Don't be silly. You hardly need me fawning all over you. You've got the rest of the town thinking you're King of the World. Don't you think that's enough?"

"For the time being," agreed Jesper loftily. Then he made a ridiculously evil face. "First Regina, then Canada, then the world! All shall bow to Jesper Isbister!"

Ella had to laugh. He was just so absurd. But he'd succeeded in lifting her mood, just a little. "Don't you think your father will have something to say about that, Mr. King of the World? I mean, if he's a duke he's not going to want his son to be grander than he is!" Ella grinned at the thought.

But this time Jesper didn't laugh with her. His face turned sad. Or was it fearful? "No, he's definitely not going to want his son," he replied bitterly. Jesper got up from the table and left the room. Ella frowned. What did *that* mean?

At ten sharp, Ella was ready. Tardiness was against the rules. Jesper was looking elegant in a light grey summer tweed suit, covered in a long coat called an auto duster. He was leaning against Mr. Barclay's gleaming new Cadillac. Jesper saw the bulge of the Brownie wrapped in Ella's sweater, but other than raising an eyebrow, did nothing to give her away. He really wasn't a bad fellow, just annoying, thought Ella gratefully. The day would be absolutely no fun without her Brownie. Not that there was likely to be much of a story at one of her mother's work parties.

"Your help today is much appreciated, Mr. Isbister," said Mrs. Barclay. "So few people know how to drive an automobile."

"It is my pleasure, Mrs. Barclay," replied Jesper, all his jauntiness back in place.

The ride to the Duncan home, where the meeting was to be held, was short. Mrs. Jennie Duncan was the pharmacist's wife, and very active in the social circles of Regina. Ella knew their son James from school, but she hoped he wouldn't be there. She'd had enough teasing for one morning.

When Mrs. Duncan's maid showed them to the parlour, the ladies already assembled stood up to greet them.

"Alex! It's so good to see you!" exclaimed Mrs. Duncan.

Alex? Who was Alex? Surely not her mother, the esteemed Mrs. Alexandra Barclay?

"Yes, Alex, we weren't sure how to parcel up the books, so we waited until you arrived," said another lady.

Ella eyes grew big. Mrs. Duncan's parlour was filled with stacks and stacks of books! She had never seen so many outside of the library. Where had they come from? What were they for? She sidled past the chattering ladies to look at the stacks, making sure she didn't touch anything. There were books for grown-ups, books for children, books about farming, religious books, and even stacks of books written in other languages. Ella couldn't even read the titles of those. She was utterly mystified.

"Ladies, ladies," called Mrs. Duncan. "Please take your seats. This meeting of the Imperial Order of the Daughters of the Empire will come to order." All the ladies sat down on straight-backed chairs. Mrs. Barclay nodded to Ella, indicating that she should sit too. She carefully placed her sweater, hiding the Brownie, beside her.

"The book drive has gone exceptionally well, as you can see. Now we need to sort through the books and make appropriate selections for all the families. Alex, do you have the list?"

Ella's mother stood up. "Ethel MacLachlan and I have been working with Mr. Sifton, Minister of the Interior, to collect the names of homesteaders in remote areas, those not close to a town library. I'll divide up the lists between you. Under each family name, you'll find the number and ages of the children in the family and the language they speak, if it isn't English, to help you with your choices. I think we have enough books to be able to send five to each family. And I've brought my daughter Ella to help select the children's books. She's a very good reader!" Ella sat straight up with pride.

"So, dive in, ladies!" Alex, although it was hard for Ella to think of her mother that way, handed out the lists. The women began to browse the stacks of books, putting together small piles for each family. Shyly, Ella sorted through the children's books, making separate piles for picture books, readers and novels. The women stopped by from time to time and asked for her advice. They told Ella about the family on their list, and she helped select the right books for the children in that family. In no time, the great stacks became neatly wrapped brown packages, each with a family name and location marked boldly on the front.

Ella couldn't resist. When no one was looking, she carefully eased the Brownie out from under her sweater and took a picture of all the packages. There were so many!

Just then, there was a honk from outside. The ladies gathered on the porch, arms full of packages. There was Jesper, sitting jauntily at the wheel of the Cadillac.

"Ladies, I have arrived to do your bidding!" he said grandly, tipping his hat. He jumped out of the car and began loading it up with all the brown paper packages of books.

"What's happening?" Ella whispered to her mother. "Why is Mr. Isbister here?"

"Mr. Sifton arranged for free delivery of all the books. Mr. Isbister will take the packages to the train so the books can be delivered to the homesteaders," her mother replied. "The women on the homesteads are very much alone, and many children are too far from a school to attend. This is not much, just a small gift to make their lives a little less lonely."

Ella was excited. This was way more important than embroidery. She looked up at her mother curiously. No, she looked up at Alex.

When the loading was done, the women made up a package of baked goods to give Jesper in thanks for his help. There was a lot of female twittering, in Ella's opinion. She was never quite sure why all the ladies liked Jesper so much. He was a perfectly okay person if he could stop teasing for ten minutes, but he wasn't special. Douglas was special. Billy was special, in a different sort of way. But Jesper? Was it his upper-class British accent? His handsome face? The fact that his father was a duke? She wondered about his bitter words at breakfast. What did he mean, that his father didn't want him? If that was true, maybe that was why Jesper loved all the attention he got in Regina. Ella found herself feeling just a little sorry for him.

The work complete, the ladies trooped back to the parlour for refreshments. As they settled down with their tea, Mrs. MacLachlan spoke up.

"Did you hear what Nellie just did, over in Winnipeg?"

"No, do tell, Ethel!" laughed the ladies. "Nellie's such a pistol!"

"Who's Nellie?" whispered Ella. Alex leaned over and whispered back, "Nellie McClung. She's a real fighter, wants the government to allow women to vote. And she's absolutely hilarious – she has the most outrageous sense of humour!"

"Well," went on Mrs. MacLachlan, "she wrote a letter to the Premier asking him to give women the vote. He said no, so she wrote a play and reversed everything. In her play, the Premier was a woman and it was men begging to be allowed to vote. And the female Premier said no, politics might upset them!"

All the ladies burst out laughing. "That Nellie!" they chortled.

Just then James came into the parlour looking for goodies, and it was just Ella's bad luck that his friends Bruce and Philip were with him. They were dressed in their Boy Scout uniforms.

"How're your knees, Ella?" asked Bruce as he stuffed two

sandwiches in his mouth. "Healed up yet? Bet that new boy still has bruises!"

"Yeah, that was a great fight!" exclaimed James loudly.

All chatter ceased. Mrs. Barclay's face went white. She wasn't Alex any more.

"What fight?" she asked quietly.

"The fight at school," said Bruce helpfully. Ella glared at him. "There's this new boy and Ella took a picture of him and he got mad and pushed her down and then the other boys fought him. It was super." James gave Bruce a dig in the ribs to make him stop. "Well, it was," replied Bruce defensively.

Mrs. Barclay turned to Ella in the silence that followed. It was clear she was furious, but Ella knew she'd hold it in until they got home. There was nothing she could say in her own defense.

Mrs. Duncan jumped in to turn the conversation around. "I wasn't aware that there was a new boy at school. It seems an odd time of year to start, with the school year ending soon."

James filled her in. "He says he's living in the Turret House, that he's a relation of old Mr. Leatherby."

"How odd," murmured the ladies, and the silence was broken. Ella said not one more word for the rest of the long painful morning.

Not until they were in their own parlour did Mrs. Barclay speak to Ella. She simply directed Ella to a chair and stared at her.

"Did I not tell you about being a busybody?" Mrs. Barclay demanded.

Ella nodded glumly.

"And now you see why?"

Ella nodded again.

"What about this boy? What kind of a person is he, if he's starting fights on his first day of school?"

Ella had to be careful not to let on that she and this 'person' were now friends. "His name is Billy Forsythe. He's from England. He says he's a poor relation. He's skinny and his clothes are awful," said Ella quietly. All that was true. "But Mother, I don't think he really wanted to fight. The other boys started it."

"The other boys?" asked Mrs. Barclay with an arched brow. "Or you, with your camera?"

Ella said nothing.

"Ella," Mrs. Barclay sighed, "If he is a poor relation, then coming to Regina is a wonderful opportunity for him. Do not stand in the way of his making something of himself. But do not include yourself either. It is not the place of a young lady to involve herself in such matters."

"But Mother, I think he needs help. After it was over, he came to apologize. He was nice. I don't think he's ever been to school, because he couldn't do any of the work. He doesn't know how to talk right, he doesn't know how to dress, or act for that matter. There is something strange about him..." Ella's thoughts scattered. "Why is helping him different from helping the homesteaders, like you did today?"

"We *can* help. I can ask George Appleby, the Scoutmaster, to invite him to join the Boy Scouts. That would certainly be an appropriate thing to do. Because a lady helps only from a distance. It is not appropriate to involve oneself intimately. Especially at your age."

Ella was going to have to think about that. Was her mother right, or was this just another rule?

Mrs. Barclay sighed. "Let me see your knees."

As her mother touched up the scrapes with iodine, Ella said quietly. "I'm glad you asked me to help today, Mother. It made me feel proud." Mrs. Barclay just smiled.

CHAPTER 5

Lunch at the Royal

"Ye daftie! What were ye thinking? Ye'll get caught!"

The boy lay on a thin pallet on the floor. He rolled over to face the wall. "I won't."

"Do ye not listen? I hear that the Mounted Police are lookin' for a runaway. A runaway what stole a man's life savings from under his mattress. It's not jest the man after ye now, boy."

"I didn't steal no life savings!"

"Ye jest stole a pair of trousers. Who's goin' ta believe ye now?"

There was silence for a moment. Then the old man spoke. "Nivver trust the lassie. She's naw our kind. She'll turn on ye, just watch."

"Why won't you talk wi' me?" Billy caught up with Ella after school as she walked across Victoria Park. "I said I was sorry. And you shook on it. We're supposed to be friends."

"We are friends," replied Ella firmly. "Just not in public."

"What – I'm not good enough for Ella whatever-fancy-last-name-you-have?" said Billy angrily. "You'll only be friends when it suits you, when nobody's looking?" Ella stared at Billy.

"You wouldn't want your mother to find out you're associatin' with the riffraff," he added sarcastically. "You wouldn't want 'er to find out you made a decision on your own, would you?"

Ella went red. Why did he always make her feel bad? Why on earth did she want to be his friend anyway?

"Good for you, but not for me," Billy went on. "Nobody else'll talk wi' me. Everybody thinks I wronged you, so until you start talkin' to me, nobody else will."

That put Ella in a pickle. What if he was right? What if everybody else was waiting for her to forgive him, in front of all the others? She'd watched him all week at school. The day after the disastrous snapshot, he'd arrived at school dressed properly, with a new scribbler and pencil. Maybe he told old Mr. Leatherby that he got into the fight because of his awful clothes. And Ella could see him copying the way the other kids talked and acted. He was watching all the time, and doing just what the others did. Taking notes in his head, almost. Even after just one week, he didn't stand out as a stranger anywhere near so much as at first. He was almost starting to blend in.

Even his schoolwork was improving. When Miss Hayward saw how much he was struggling, she'd asked him right out if he'd ever been to school before. And bold as brass, he'd said, "No, ma'am. This be me first week." After that, she set him easy problems and he was progressing quickly, now that he was starting at the beginning like you were supposed to.

"All right," said Ella decisively, changing her mind yet again. "Tomorrow I will eat lunch with you. In public. All right?"

Billy grinned. "All right! See you tomorrow!" Then he ran past her on his way to the Turret House, turning once to wave.

After school, Ella picked up her pictures from the pharmacy. Luckily, Mr. Duncan didn't comment. Maybe he hadn't looked at them, at least, she hoped he hadn't. Ella hurried home.

Safe in her bedroom with the door closed, she laid out the pictures. Oh, my. They were as bad as she'd thought. She looked ridiculous down on her knees and even her tears showed in the photo. She was mortified, but the picture of the fight was actually rather exciting. It definitely told a story. Too bad she couldn't show it to anyone. Hiding the two photos in her underwear drawer, Ella collected the other four and went to find her father in his study. He beckoned her in.

"Hmm," he said as she spread the photos across his desk. "What do you think, Ella?"

"The picture of my classmates was hard to take," she began. "They kept moving around and it was hard to get them to fit into the frame."

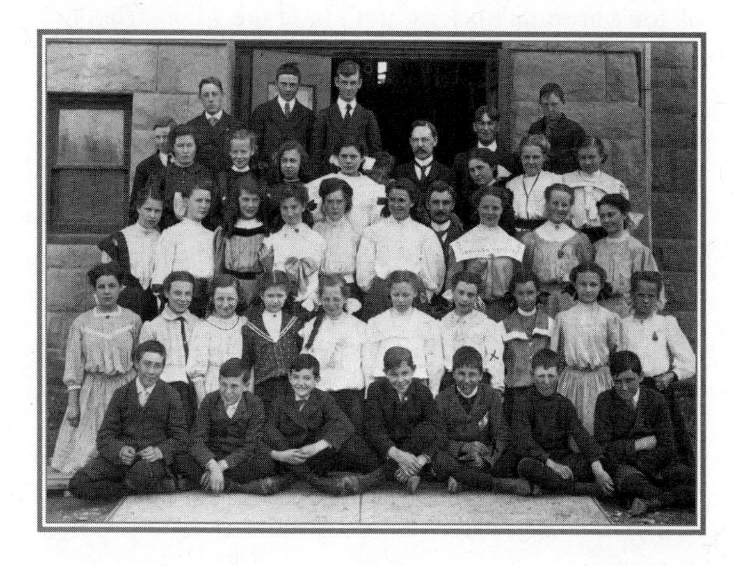

"Yes, that's true. Group photos are very difficult. But I think you've done a fine job with this. Can you see the story?"

Ella frowned at the picture. "I wasn't looking for a story. I was only looking for the people," she replied.

"Yes, but it's the people who tell the story," smiled Mr. Barclay. "See here? That boy in front – I bet he's a rascal." Ella grinned. Jimmy was the class clown. "And the older girl in the dark blouse – see how's she's standing? She wants the boys to look at her; she's flirting with the camera." It was true! Ella was amazed. Harriet was always talking to the boys. "And this young man, here at the back," said Mr. Barclay, pointing at the top right corner. "He's definitely a story. He's holding himself apart, as if he doesn't want to be a part of the group, or is perhaps afraid."

Ella caught her breath. It was Billy. Her father saw it too!

"Look, Daddy, here's another picture of that boy. You said to look for what didn't belong and out of the whole schoolyard, I picked him!"

"Good girl!" said Mr. Barclay proudly. "You're getting it. What about these other photos?" Together they looked at the picture of the fountain and the packages of books.

"They aren't very interesting," said Ella in disappointment.

"Oh, but they are," replied her father. "Here's your second lesson. Close your eyes. Tell me what's in the picture of the fountain."

Ella closed her eyes and thought. "Just the fountain," she said.

"Not just the fountain. Look again." Ella opened her eyes and looked at the picture again. Behind the fountain the man was throwing a ball for his white dog. Off to the side, a little girl was clutching her mother's long skirt, afraid of the dog. A mounted police officer was riding his horse down the road in the background. And if she looked really closely she could see...yes, it was Harriet and she was kissing a boy behind a bush!

Mr. Barclay laughed. "When we look around us, we don't see half of what's there. A picture captures everything. It tells us the story behind the story and gives us time to appreciate it." Mr. Barclay looked at the picture of the parcels of books.

"You're lucky your mother didn't catch you snapping this, young lady," he said sternly. Ella sighed.

"She really doesn't like the camera," replied Ella sadly.

"And do you know why?" She shook her head. "Ella, your mother is like a photograph. There is far more to her than you will ever see just by looking. I think she will surprise you one day."

The next day Ella took her lunch pail and bravely walked right past the rest of her friends, who were gathered in their favourite corner of the schoolyard to eat. They stared. Ella headed to the fencepost where Billy was waiting, a big grin on his face. Before she sat down, she said in a loud voice so everybody could hear, "I forgive you for making me fall." Then she sat down and lifted the lid of her pail.

For a moment, all heads were turned their way. But just for a moment. Then everybody went back to eating lunch. It was done.

"Where's your lunch?" asked Ella.

"Oh, I don't bring one," replied Billy quickly. "I get such a big dinner at night, I'm never hungry at lunchtime."

"My," said Ella. "That must be a huge dinner! Really, you should eat more, you know. You're too skinny. Take this." She handed him an apple. Billy hesitated a moment, then took it. He took the first bite slowly, then practically inhaled the rest of it.

"You even ate the core! See, you are hungry at lunch," laughed Ella. "Does Mr. Leatherby have a cook? He must. Get her to pack you something every day. If you're not hungry, you don't have to eat it."

"I don't think she likes me," said Billy with a scowl. "On the weekends, I get my own dinner. I like Chinese food the best. Do you?"

"Chinese food?! Where do you get it? Oh, you don't go to the Royal Restaurant, do you? That's not allowed!"

"Why isn't it allowed?" asked Billy curiously. "The food's really tasty."

"Because you're not supposed to go there! Those people come from far away, you know. And they don't clean properly. They eat things that aren't fit for humans. Everybody knows that."

Billy stared at Ella. "That's the craziest thing I ever heard in my life. Best food I ever et, and there ain't a speck o' dirt anywhere in that place. You should come, so's you can see for yerself."

Go to the Royal?! She couldn't! Her mother's voice rang like a bell in her head. Young ladies do not chew food in public. White people do not eat foreign food. There were so many rules.

Ella made a decision. "I'll go!"

The following Saturday Ella dressed carefully. "Goodbye, Mother," she called out. Mrs. Barclay materialized at the front door.

"Where exactly are you going? When will you be back? Who is going with you?"

Ella bit her lip. "I'm meeting a friend from school," she replied carefully. "We're going to the library to study." She took a big breath. "It's the new boy." Ella waited for an explosion. It wasn't long in coming.

"What did I tell you about that boy?!" said Mrs. Barclay in a tight voice. "Spending time with him is not appropriate."

Ella was ready with her explanation of how nobody would accept him until she did. "I'm just trying not to stand in his way, Mother."

"You're just trying to twist my words, young lady. This family has a reputation..." Mrs. Barclay was forced to stop when the doorbell rang. Mrs. Barclay's lips tightened.

Mrs. Dudek ushered Billy into the parlour. Ella gaped; he was hardly recognizable. His new trousers were brushed clean, his old boots were blackened, and someone had taken scissors to his hair. He looked clean and neat and almost respectable. To Ella's amusement, he bowed low to her mother.

"My name is Billy Forsythe, ma'am. I appreciate being allowed to go to the library with your daughter. I am a poor boy from England. She is helping me fit in at school and get better at my studies. I am very grateful." He'd clearly practiced this speech. Ella had to clap her hand over her mouth to stop from giggling.

Mrs. Barclay's lip twitched at his formality. He was trying so hard.

"Hello, Billy. It's nice to meet you. Would you please excuse us for a moment?" Mrs. Barclay nodded to Ella, indicating that she should follow her. They left Billy in the parlour.

"This is not appropriate. I can see the young man's appeal, but really, what do we know of him?"

"Mother, I'm just helping a schoolmate. He's way behind in math and you know that's my best subject." Ella fired her best shot: "You didn't mind when I went to the library to help Douglas. And he's older than me!"

"That was a completely different situation. We know Douglas's family. I'm not happy, but it would be rude to refuse the young man now. Ella, be careful. And be home and washed, ready for dinner at six o'clock." Then she added ominously, "We will continue this discussion later." Ella sighed. That didn't sound good.

"Yes, Mother," said Ella. They walked back to the parlour, nearly bumping into Jesper in the hall.

Mrs. Barclay jumped. "Mr. Isbister, you startled me!"

"My sincere apologies, Mrs. Barclay. Miss Barclay." Jesper tipped his hat and went out the front door, but not until he had stared hard at Billy, who was standing in the doorway of the parlour staring right back.

Ella felt uncomfortable – and strong. She didn't like lying to her mother, but it felt right to be friends with Billy. It was so confusing.

When they turned the corner onto Lorne Street, Billy looked at Ella. "Last chance to back out."

"No," said Ella firmly. "It's time I started making up my own mind about things." They turned up the street towards the Royal Restaurant.

"Are you scared?" Billy grinned.

"Never," Ella replied, but that was her second lie of the day. When they got to the Royal, the same Chinese man she'd seen in the alley was waiting for them. He was dressed in baggy black trousers and a loose brocade jacket with a high collar. His long black hair was braided into a pigtail that hung down his back, and was topped by a strange looking beanie with a pompom on the top. He bowed low to Ella. She was shaking. She'd never been so close to a foreigner before. Mrs. Dudek didn't count.

"Please, please, this way, special place for you," he said, bowing over and over again. Ella wasn't sure if she was supposed to bow too, so she just gave the man a weak smile. He led them to a table in the back.

"I didn't think you'd want to be seen through the window," whispered Billy. "I asked Hong to put us here."

"Hong?" asked Ella.

"That's his name. He and his brother Li own the restaurant. Li's wife cooks, and their kids wash dishes. The whole family works here."

"That's terrible!" exclaimed Ella indignantly. "Children shouldn't be working! They should be in school."

"Lots of kids work, Ella," Billy said quietly. "You only get to go to school if your family has enough money to buy food. Otherwise, you've got to help or you all starve."

That caught Ella up short. "Did you ever have to work?"

"Yeah, I've worked. Why d'you think me mam sent me here?"

"Oh." Ella thought hard. "So she sent you to your uncle so you could go to school and not have to work any more?"

Billy gave her another long look. "Somethin' like that."

Hong arrived just then, carrying steaming plates of food. "Chickee," he said, pointing at one dish. "Duck. Bok choi. Shiitake. Wonton soup. Egg roll." Ella felt her stomach heave. She'd never heard of such food. Was it even edible? He lifted the lid of a woven wooden basket. "Rice. All good, good. Best in house. Eat. Eat!" He handed each of them two long wooden sticks and hurried away. "Do we have to eat with our hands?" whispered Ella.

Billy laughed. "No, like this." He showed her how to use the chopsticks. Ella was amazed. How could people eat without forks? Finally Hong took pity on her feeble attempts and brought her a utensil she recognized. Ella smiled gratefully, and gingerly took her first bite.

It was delicious!

Billy was right – it was the best food in the world. Ella ate and ate as if she would never stop. Hong kept bringing more food, his grin bigger each time he came to the table. Finally they could eat no more. Hong brought tea in the tiniest teacup she had ever seen.

"Milk?" she asked.

"No milkee, bad, bad," frowned Hong. Ella tasted the tea. Hong was right. It tasted better without.

"That was wonderful," Ella said as she leaned back in her chair. "And everything is spotless, just like you said."

"You need to see with your own eyes," replied Billy. "Or with this!" For the second time he grabbed her Brownie, only this time she didn't mind. "Hong," he called. The Chinese man came rushing to the table. "Can we take your picture?" Hong bowed several times, making his pigtail bounce up and down. Then he stood straight and put a severe look on his face. Ella had to laugh.

"No, Hong!" she said. "You're supposed to smile!" Hong looked a little confused, but did as she asked. Billy pushed the button.

There was a commotion at the door.

"I have to play!"

Ella recognized that voice. It belonged to Jesper. But what was he doing at the Royal? Had he followed her? Ella shrank down in her seat, hoping for invisibility. At that moment, three things happened at once. Another Chinese man came up from the basement and angrily grabbed Jesper's arm. Billy snapped a picture. And Jesper saw Ella.

CHAPTER 6

The Prairie

"Let go of me!" shouted Jesper. He shook his arm free, nearly pushing the Chinese man down the stairs and losing his hat in the process. "Don't you know who I am?"

Jesper looked about ready to explode. He was so angry. As Ella stared at him, he took a deep breath, straightened his expression, then bent down and retrieved his hat.

"Miss Barclay, what a surprise. Does your mother know you are here?"

Ella was caught.

"And your companion? Certainly not a young man of any class. Really, Miss Barclay, is this wise?" The two Chinese men, Hong and presumably his brother Li, frowned.

Ella's surprise had turned to dismay and was moving right on to fear. Jesper was acting like some other person, somebody she didn't even know. "Billy is my friend, Mr. Isbister," she replied with more confidence than she actually felt. "We're eating lunch."

"In an establishment such as this? Really, Miss Barclay, I thought you knew better." Jesper glared. A stray thought jumped into Ella's head. Without the smile, he wasn't really handsome at all.

"Mr. Isbister, why are *you* here?" she asked cautiously.

"That is certainly none of your affair, young lady. But if you must know, it is financial business. You wouldn't understand. Now, I suggest you leave immediately and go straight home." His expression relaxed. He looked more like the Jesper she thought she knew. "I understand rebellion, Ella," he went on, quietly so only she could hear. "I won't tell your mother. But don't come here again. It's dangerous."

Dangerous?

Hong escorted them to the door. He looked sad. Billy reached into his pocket and pulled out two meal tickets. Hong waved them away. "No tickee, no tickee. Hong happy happy you like food. So sorry for bad man coming. So sorry. Please come back." He bowed low.

Ella was shaking. She was in so much trouble. Billy was embarrassed. Neither one knew what to say. Somebody had to break the silence.

"I'm so sorry, Ella. I didn't mean for that to 'appen."

"Not your fault," murmured Ella. "Just bad luck." They walked aimlessly for a block.

"What did he mean saying Hong's place was dangerous? Will the food make me sick?"

Billy had to laugh. "Good food like that? Never," he replied. "Surely you've 'eard what goes on in the basement of the Royal?"

"What do you mean?" asked Ella.

"It's a gambling den!" whispered Billy. "Didn't you 'ear your boarder say he wanted 'to play'? He must be a gambler!"

"That's utterly ridiculous!" Ella snorted. "Why would Jesper gamble? He has tons of money."

"Gambling ain't always about the money. It's about the game. Some blokes can't stop themselves from playing. Anyway," Billy went on, "look at it this way, Ella. If he's a gambler, you're safe. He'll never tell anybody he saw you at the Royal."

Ella cocked her head. That did make her feel better. She almost hoped Mr. Isbister *was* a gambler, just for her own sake. "Oh look, Billy!"

They'd walked almost to the railway tracks. Ella hardly ever went there; young ladies just didn't. There were too many burly men with roving eyes. But it wasn't the trains or the men that had caught Ella's eye.

"Look at the horses!"

Billy smiled. "That's the Palace Livery Stable. I know some of the blokes as work there. Want to meet the 'orses?"

Ella's eyes shone. Would she?! Before her father bought the Cadillac, they'd had a lovely horse named Cleo to pull their buggy. Her father always said that when she was old enough he'd teach her to ride. But then he bought the motorcar and sold Cleo. Mrs. Barclay said riding skills were no longer required for a young girl destined to live in the city, so that was the end of that.

Up close, the horses seemed huge. "This 'ere's Martha. She's old and slow and she likes carrots." Billy handed Ella a carrot from a nearby basket. "You can feed her if you want." Ella giggled with delight when Martha's sensitive lips wrapped around the carrot, and pulled her hand back quickly when she saw the huge teeth.

"Hey, Forsythe," called out Mr. Mulligan, owner of the livery stable. "Whatcha up to?"

"Just visitin'," replied Billy. "This 'ere's Ella."

Mr. Mulligan tipped his hat. "Hello, Miss. You like old Martha here?"

Ella nodded enthusiastically. "Hey, Forsythe, wanta take her for a walk? She walks so darn slow the rest of us ain't got time and she's restless. You know she's our weather vane and she's actin' like there's a storm coming. But this time I'm sure the old girl is wrong. It's too hot and sunny to rain. But I guess she don't know that."

" 'Appy to, but Ella don't know 'ow to ride," explained Billy. His speech was falling into old patterns, Ella noticed. He sounded just like a worker, not a schoolboy.

"Go ahead, hitch her up to the old buggy there. You'd be doing us a favour, boy."

Ella grinned in delight. What fun! She forgot about the incident at the Royal completely as she watched Billy hitch Martha to the buggy. He certainly knew what he was doing. Mr. Leatherby didn't have any horses, so Billy must have had some back in England. Otherwise he wouldn't know what to do.

In no time they were clip-clopping down the road towards Albert Street. Billy turned right and headed north out of town. Their route took them into the Warehouse District. Ella looked around with interest. She'd never seen it before today. Come to that, her whole day seemed to be a series of first times. First big lie, first meal in a restaurant, first taste of Chinese food... Ella felt exhilarated.

"Ella," said Billy cautiously, as they clopped along the road. "Would you like to meet a friend of mine?"

"Who?" asked Ella cautiously. She already knew all the kids from school.

"His name's Jock. He's kind of old, but he tells great stories. He lives around here and I bet he'd like a ride in a buggy."

Ella caught her breath. She couldn't. Bad enough she was out alone with Billy. She'd *never* be forgiven if her mother found out a man had been with her as well. But before Ella could figure out how to say that to Billy, he was turning onto Dewdney Avenue, right into the Warehouse District.

"Please, Ella? He's a grand bloke. I know you'll like him."

Ella swallowed. She'd do it! On this day of firsts, she decided she was prepared to do anything.

Billy led Martha past several warehouses and two taverns. *My goodness,* thought Ella. *Real taverns!* Many of the buildings were new, and some were imposing. The buildings weren't out of place. *She* was, and that was the story. She felt like an explorer. Ella snapped a photo, wishing she could be in it just to prove that she'd been there.

Tucked neatly in the shadow of the Ackerman Building was a small wooden house. Although it was two storeys tall, the whole house only reached as high as the first floor of the imposing Ackerman Building. Billy pulled on the reins in front of the house. "Whoa, Martha," he said gently.

Billy helped Ella down from the buggy and led her towards

the house. Ella clasped her hands primly and tried to look like her mother, straight and tall and proper. She didn't want any of the Warehouse District men thinking they could speak with her. She'd be terrified to death. But the men on the street either didn't notice her or merely gave her a polite nod. Perhaps the Warehouse District wasn't as terrible as she'd been told? Billy knocked on the door. It was opened by an odd little man with a startled look on his face.

"Billy?" the man said in surprise.

"Jock, this is Ella Barclay. Ella, this is my friend Jock Ballogh."

The look of shock on Ella's face was mirrored on Jock's. Wide-eyed, Jock turned to Billy, who was looking nervous.

What ye doing, boy? This ain't right!

As for Ella, she didn't know what to do. Young ladies were not allowed to meet strange men without a chaperone. Should she shake hands? Speak? How on earth had she come to be here? Not a single one of her mother's rules told her what to do next. Jock recovered first and gave an elaborate bow.

"My dear young lady," he said a little too grandly. "I am verra pleased to make yer acquaintance."

Ella gave Jock a nervous smile. "As I am yours, Mr. Ballogh," she replied politely.

"No need for any Misters 'round here," the man said cautiously. "I'm jest Jock, always have been. Sit ye doon."

Ella took a closer look. Jock wasn't a big man. He was very thin, like Billy, and looked wiry. He wore a white shirt that her mother would have turned down for rags, but it was clean, at least. His dungarees were rolled up almost to his knees and he wore thick knitted socks stuffed into worn leather boots. The dungarees were held up with a rope belt, just as Billy's had been that very first day. He wore a jaunty red bandana knotted round his neck, and his grizzled hair had been razored close to his head. Jock's most distinguishing feature, however, was his huge moustache. Ella had never seen the like. It stuck straight out from both sides of his upper lip, then curled up in a twist at the ends. It was shiny with wax and when he smiled, the moustache tilted so that the twirly ends nearly touched his eyebrows. Ella couldn't take her eyes off it. How did Billy ever meet such a man?

Jock was over his shock. He spied her Brownie. He grinned. "Can ye took me photey?" he asked. "Billy tol' me ye wiz a photeygrapher. I ain't nivver had a photeygraph," he went on. "And I ain't got nuthin' to hide, not like some as shoud nivver uv got his photey took," he said pointedly, looking at Billy. Billy looked defiantly back. Ella didn't understand the looks that passed between them. But it didn't matter. She was too busy savouring the words, "You are a photographer." *I'm not just Ella*, she thought to herself. *I'm something more.* She took Jock's picture.

Jock liked the idea of a buggy ride. "Take me oot to see me woman!" he grinned. "'Tis time for a visit!"

Ella frowned. What was he talking about? Billy was grinning right back at Jock. She felt left out of the joke.

They all trooped back out to Martha, and Jock hopped into the back of the buggy. Clearly Jock wasn't as old as she'd first thought. It was just that he looked so worn out and tired. He was probably younger than her father. And he talked strangely, with an accent she had never heard before.

Martha led them past the grain elevator right out of the city. Billy and Jock chatted together. Ella was content to look around in wonder. The sky was a perfect blue with not a cloud in sight. As far as Ella could see were acres and acres of wheat, waving back and forth with the prairie breeze. It made her feel like swaying in time with it, as if she was part of a lullaby. She wanted to climb out of the buggy, lie down and pull the blanket of wheat around her so she could see the blue, blue sky through a lattice of green.

Billy laughed when she told him. "The ground is hard. The wheat isn't soft, it's scratchy, and you'd be sneezing like a crazy woman from all the dust in two minutes!"

Ella didn't care. It looked luxurious. She heard a sound. "What's that?" she asked. "It's beautiful."

Billy listened. "I dunno."

"Daft lad!" laughed Jock. "It's a meadowlark. Look around ye – he'll probably be sittin' on a fence post." Ella looked. She couldn't even see a fence post, much less a bird in all that wheat. Then she caught a flicker of movement. "There!" she pointed.

"Is he singing for his lady? He looks like a knight in shining armour!"

Billy snorted. True, the meadowlark had a golden breast and its song was one of the most beautiful in the world. But all was never as it seemed. Jock explained.

"He's singin' to defend his woman, young Ella. He wilnae giv 'er up. An' he'll fight like a banshee iffen anuvver bird stops by. They'll lock their feet and roll 'round the ground and stab wit their beaks, dinnae think they won't. Most of us creatures in this world havta fight to get whit they want, nivver mind how beautiful."

"Mr. Ballogh...I mean, Jock, where do you come from?" Ella asked shyly.

"From Cowcaddens, lassie," replied Jock. "That'd be in Glasgow, in Scotland."

"Why did you come here?" Ella persisted. "Scotland is so far away!"

"'Tis that," replied Jock. "But it's not a bonny place, Cowcaddens, I'll tell you that. Most fellas be lucky ta get oot. Meself, I saw the Canada Exhibition Wagon and come oot the next boat."

"What's the Canada Exhibition Wagon?" asked Ella curiously.

"A wondrous thing, to be sure!" laughed Jock. "Convinced men smarter'n meself to come to this land. Young Ella, it was a Gaso-Electrical vehicle, didn't need naw horses to pull it. D'ye fancy that! So me pals and meself, we crowded 'round to see this contraption, close enough ta read the signs painted aboot the wagon. Ah, pure excitement them signs caused!"

"What did they say?" Ella was fascinated by his story.

"They said, 'Send your boys to Canada. All males over eighteen years of age entitled to 160 acres free farm lands in Western Canada.' Dinnae think it didna sound like heaven to us lads, I'll tell ye. Then it got better."

"What happened?" breathed Ella.

"Why lassie, they opened up the side of that wagon, right before our eyes. And inside was a display the like of which we'd never seen in our lives!"

"What was in it?"

"Sheaves of wheat, and great jars of honey. Stuffed rabbits and a buffalo head! There was baked bread and baskets of eggs – more food than we'd see in a month. And all free for the takin' in Canada for a man willing ta work, they said. Now, in Cowcaddens, we lived twelve inna room and were starved most o' the time. Couldnae see a tree or a blade o'grass any way we looked. That's a far sight different from 160 acres of free farm lands. An' we was willing to work. Canada seemed a pretty fine idea to us then. So we hopped on the next boat, fast as a punter runnin' from the mob."

Ella thought of the tiny house beside the Ackerman Building. Jock clearly wasn't living on 160 acres of land. "Did they not give you the free land?" she asked cautiously.

"Aye, they did, lassie. Tied a ribbon on my wagon wheel, told me how many turns of the wheel it would take to get to me land, and there it be, pretty as ye please. Loved that land, I did," sighed Jock. "But it was too much for me. Seems that a bloke from Cowcaddens dinnae necessarily make the best farmer. I'm a city boy, I guess. Best off in Regina."

"I'm not," said Billy. "I love it out here!" He turned to Ella and his expression became serious. "I want to be a farmer. A real homesteader. But I can't apply for my 160 acres until I'm eighteen. Me mam wanted me to be educated, so I'm spending me waitin' time at school to please her, but it's the land that's important." He turned to Ella, his face alight.

"You understand, don't you? Because isn't this the most beautiful place you ever saw?"

CHAPTER 7

Accusations

The boy's talkin' like a daftie. It's dangerous. And the girl's not strong. She can't help him if folks start askin' questions. And she's the one with the photeygraph. This is goin' to be trouble. Where'll I be if he gets taken away?

Jock shook his head. What was done was done. Nuthin' he could do. He decided to take a nap.

Billy clicked his tongue to start Martha up. "This isn't like England. There it was dark and gloomy. Where I lived, people starved. There was no hope. But here in Canada you have all that anybody could ever want." Billy stood up in the buggy and shouted. "I want it too!"

Ella applauded. "You're lucky to know what you want," she said. "I don't."

Billy poked her in the ribs. "You don't need to know, my lady Ella. You're rich – you're allowed to want everything." Billy stopped the buggy, jumped down and grabbed a handful of wheat. Deftly he twisted the stalks into a braided ring, climbed back into the buggy and placed it on Ella's head with great ceremony.

"Ella, Queen of the Wheat," he intoned, and bowed low. Ella couldn't help but laugh.

She punched him on the arm. "You're making fun of me."

"Yup," he said blithely, not bothered at all. Then he hopped out of the buggy again and reached up to help Ella down. "Race you!" They ran through the waving rows of wheat until Ella had to stop and clutch her side. "Enough, you win!" she laughed. She dropped to her knees and lay down in the wheat, scratchy or not.

Billy lay down beside her. "On my land, I won't just plant wheat. I'll plant flax too, for the oil. And because it's pretty – the whole field turns blue when the flax flowers, as blue as your eyes, Ella, can you believe it? And I'll raise horses, of course. And build a sod house." Billy hopped up and threw his arms towards the sun. "It's the best land in the world!" He was so funny, Ella couldn't help herself. She snapped another picture of Billy.

Slowly they walked back to the buggy. Jock had his red bandana over his face and was happily snoring in the back of the buggy. Reluctantly, they turned Martha around. Ella felt full, expanded, as if her whole body had grown to fit the wide open space. There was a comfortable silence.

"What's that?" Billy pointed.

Ella peered across the sunny prairie. "That's my daddy's Cadillac!" she said. "What's it doing in the middle of the field?"

"Let's check," said Billy, and he pulled on Martha's reins. As they drew closer to the car, they could hear laughing and talking. A group of young men were huddled around the car, smoking, and yes, some of them were drinking too.

"Nobody," said Jock dismissively, poking his head up from the back of the buggy. "Jest a bunch of no-good Remittance Men."

"Remittance Men?" asked Ella curiously.

"Aye. Rich fellas from England. Come here for a piece of all this, but their folks back home send 'em money every month so they dinnae hafta work. D'ye ken whit I think?" he went on with derision in his voice. "They nivver grow up to be real men."

Ella twisted in her seat so she could keep watching. "So if they're Remittance Men," she said slowly, "why is Mr. Isbister out here with them?"

Billy's eyes narrowed. For the third time, he grabbed Ella's Brownie, twisted in his seat and pushed the button.

"Do you think they can see us?" asked Ella nervously. "If Mr. Isbister sees me out here, I'll be in even more trouble!"

"Seems to me *he* oughta be in terrible trouble for taking your daddy's Cadillac and showing off to his friends," murmured Billy. "Don't worry, Ella, we'll go the other way."

As Martha slowly made her way back to the city, Jock could tell the sunshine had gone out of the youngsters. He sighed. There was nothing but trouble ahead, he knew that for a fact, but why not enjoy a few smiles while you waited for disaster to rain down on your head?

"Lassie," he said, "you ever seed a Gorbey?"

"What's a Gorbey?" asked Ella in surprise. She'd never heard of such a thing.

"A whiskey-jack? A camp robber?"

"What?" Ella was confused.

"Och!" said Jock jovially. "Then you never seed a Canada Jay!"

Ella looked at Billy. He shrugged his shoulders, but he was wearing a big grin.

"It's a bird, then?" she asked.

"Nivver jes any bird, lassie. This bird's *magic*."

Ella frowned. "You're spoofing me, Jock Ballogh!"

"Nivver!" he replied, hand to his heart. "This here story's all true, I swear. See, the Canada Jay lives in the spruce forests north a' here. That's where my land be, when I had it, jest next to the forest. And the Canada Jays, the Gorbeys, they was all over. Pretty little birds, and terrible clever. They stay here in winter, see, and they have to store enough food in summer to last until the snow melts in the spring. Every day, all summer, a Gorbey works like a demon, findin' food and caching it, here, there and everywhere. Thousands of caches and the Gorbey remembers *every single one*. If that ain't magic, I don't know what is. But that's not the only magic."

Jock's voice went all low and conspiratorial. "They's called camp robbers 'cause they like people food as well. And they'll come sit right on your hand if you'll give 'em a nibble. Woodsmen, they say a Gorbey will pick a piece of bacon right outa a frypan, if you're not careful. And they also say this – never, ever, neglect to share with a Gorbey. 'Cause iffen you do, trouble will come to you. That's the real magic."

"What kind of trouble can a bird cause?" asked Ella suspiciously.

"Well," replied Jock, his bright eyes gleaming, "I heard tell of a nasty man who caught a Gorbey stealin' a bite o' his breakfast and decided to punish it. He plucked every last feather from that bird and let it fly away stark naked. Next morning, that fella woke up with no hair!"

Ella burst out laughing. "That's ridiculous!"

" 'Tis true!" insisted Jock. The sunshine was back in the day. "D'ye fancy a poem?" Jock recited cowboy poems until they were all laughing. Then he began singing the old cowboy's lament, "Oh bury me not on the lone prairie," in an exaggerated voice so mournful it was hilarious. The laughter didn't stop until Dewdney Avenue.

Billy pulled on Martha's reins in front of Jock's house. "Thank you for the stories, Jock Ballogh," said Ella politely.

"Lassie, 'tis me pleasure. G'night, Billy." And Jock was off.

Billy turned Martha around. He didn't stop at the Palace Livery but continued on down Albert Street to 12th Avenue, letting Ella off on the other side of Victoria Park, close to home but not where her parents could see.

"Goodbye, Billy," said Ella, her eyes shining. "Thank you for the lovely day."

"Don't forget your crown," he said, holding it out.

"I can't keep it, Billy, you know that," she said quietly. And she walked away, leaving Billy with the crown and not much else.

The house was quiet. She wasn't late, but she would have to hurry her washing up to be ready for dinner on time. Ella had only taken the first step upstairs when she heard her father's voice.

"Come here, Ella," he said sternly.

Did they know?

Mr. Barclay, Mrs. Barclay and Jesper Isbister were all sitting stiffly in the parlour. Ella had a brief moment of surprise. How did Jesper get back from the prairie so quickly? And he looked all neat and tidy, not at all like someone who'd been smoking with his friends in the middle of a prairie field. She sat where her father pointed.

"We have a situation," Mr. Barclay said grimly. "There has been a theft." Ella started. A theft?

"A theft of money. From this house. Today."

Ella looked at her mother. Mrs. Barclay sat with her head bowed, hands clutching a handkerchief.

"Ella, who is Billy Forsythe?"

Ella was speechless. A theft? And they thought Billy had done it? But that was ridiculous. She'd been with him all day. He had a rich uncle. He didn't need to steal. *Or did he?*

Mr. Leatherby sounded cruel. And the cook didn't feed him properly. Billy knew about gambling. And what about Jock Ballogh? How could Billy know anybody in the Warehouse District?

Billy didn't mind breaking rules.

Ella had to admit that was what she liked about him. But had he gone too far? Still overwhelmed by all that had happened that day, more than had happened in her whole ordinary existence, Ella couldn't think straight. But her heart told her no. No, he didn't do it. Ella lifted her head and looked at her father.

"Billy is a poor relation from England, but a good boy. He didn't do it. I know he didn't because," Ella swallowed, "I was with him all day."

"We know," said Mrs. Barclay, her voice full of outrage. "Mr. Isbister told us he saw you at the *Royal Restaurant!*"

Ella glared at Jesper. He'd promised! Jesper had a hangdog look on his face.

"I'm sorry, Ella, but I had no choice. Under the circumstances. After all, I saw Billy in the parlour this morning. He was alone, and that's where your mother's purse was." Ella was furious. Maybe she should tattle about the Remittance Men and the Cadillac? Then his words registered. Her mother's purse?

Ella looked aghast at her mother. "He stole money from *you?*"

"Yes," replied Mrs. Barclay with dismay. "Money that belonged to the IODE. Money that was meant to buy more books."

"He didn't steal it, Daddy, I know he didn't," said Ella firmly.

"How do you know?" asked Mr. Barclay. "Do you have proof?"

"I just know, Daddy. He wouldn't – couldn't. There's another thief out there and we have to find him!"

"For heaven's sake, Ella, where is your logic? He was the only one in the parlour; Isbister can attest to that. It can't be anyone else!"

"But Daddy..."

"Stop, Ella. Loyalty is one thing, but foolishness is quite another. And this may not be the only theft, you know. There's been talk at work about a recent theft of clothing and school supplies from the Regina Trading Company. The police will want to look into this young man."

Ella could remember her exact words. *Try for a pair of trousers that fit too.* And then he came to school wearing new trousers.

And socks. She'd teased him because he had no socks. Tears began to roll down her cheeks. She couldn't help it.

"Tears won't help!" Mr. Barclay's voice began to rise in volume. "You lied to your mother today, which is a terrible offense. You visited the Chinese. This will not be tolerated!"

Ella shrank from her father. She had never seen him so angry. Usually it was her mother who punished her, never her father. She didn't like it, not one bit. He was scary. What would happen if he found out about the Warehouse District and Jock?

"You will not associate with this boy again!"

"I promise, Father," she said in a small voice. Mr. Barclay took a deep breath.

"Go wash for dinner," he said gruffly, and left the room. Mrs. Barclay followed him. She didn't look at Ella. Jesper left too, catching her eye as he went. "*Sorry*," he mouthed. Ella nodded. It wasn't his fault. Slowly she made her way upstairs.

Alone in her room, she hugged herself tightly, trying to keep the happy memories of the day from spilling out and vanishing. Would her father talk to the police? She couldn't believe that Billy was a thief, she just couldn't.

The next day was hot. Just the same, Ella didn't leave her room. She couldn't face the world. The only place for her was under the covers with her pillow over her head.

Luckily, she had math to study. Numbers were the only things that made sense, with the rest of her world so confusing. There was just one week left of school, during which the senior students would write provincial examinations in all their subjects.

That was all right with Ella. No examination could be as difficult as solving the problem of Billy.

At Sunday dinner Mrs. Barclay announced that Ella would be spending much of the next week after school helping the ladies of the IODE decorate the city for Dominion Day. The following week, on July 1st, the whole of the country would celebrate the anniversary of the day Canada became a nation. Saskatchewan had only become a province of Canada seven years earlier, so the holiday was still new in Regina and the ladies were determined to make it a grand one. That meant bunting and ribbons and electric lights, the town band and no end of festivities. Certainly there was a lot to be done, but Ella was old enough to know that her mother just wanted to keep an eye on her. But she still had to see Billy at school. Was he a thief? Or not? Whatever would she say to him?

In the end, it was easy. She said nothing. She pretended he didn't exist. No matter what Billy did to catch her eye, she ignored it. She tucked the film of their Saturday adventures away in a drawer. What was the point of developing the pictures? It wasn't as if she could show them to her father anyway.

Luckily, there was lots of chatter in the schoolyard to cover her silence. Everyone became more and more gleeful as each provincial examination ended and was delivered to the Department of Education at the Legislative Building for grading. Great plans were made for a "School's Out" party at Wascana Lake on Sunday.

"It's so hot!" said a ten-year-old boy named Leonard. "I'm going to swim clear across the lake!" Bruce and Philip decided to take their canoe. The girls planned a picnic feast. They all agreed to meet at the pergola by the lake at noon, right after church services. Everyone was coming, everyone but Billy. Only Ella thought about asking him, and she sealed her lips shut.

As Sunday drew closer, the heat grew worse. So did the humidity. Ella felt sticky and sweaty, and if she complained she just knew her mother would say that young ladies didn't sweat. Truly, if she had to hang one more string of decorative lights around Victoria Park, she thought she'd scream. There were *thousands* of them, for heaven's sake! Oh, it was hot. She couldn't wait for the picnic. She put a new film into her Brownie so she could take pictures of her friends at the lake. She packed her swimming costume: navy blue with short sleeves, a sailor collar and puffy bloomers to go underneath. It came with long black swimming stockings and even a bathing cap with a jaunty rosette. Ella was determined to jump into the lake and just stay there all afternoon. It was too hot to do anything else. It was too hot even to think.

Douglas was coming. Maybe she'd get up the nerve to talk to him, anything to forget about Billy. Ella couldn't ever remember feeling so out of sorts. Thief or not? Friend or not? Her thoughts were whirling in confusion.

Finally Sunday came. Ella's father drove her to the lake in his Cadillac so she wouldn't have to carry the heavy picnic basket Mrs. Dudek had prepared. But really, he was looking for Billy. Ella could tell. Mr. Barclay wanted to make sure he wasn't there, having fun like all the other kids. As they passed the Turret House, Ella wondered what Billy *was* doing.

"Come straight home, Ella," said Mr. Barclay. "Be home by six o'clock."

Ella nodded to her father, then trudged towards her friends. She still felt grumpy, but she did her best to get into the spirit of the picnic. After everybody changed into bathing costumes, Ella lined her friends up for a photo. Up to their knees in the lake, all the girls linked arms and grinned at the camera. Then Ella put her Brownie safely out of harm's way and ran to the edge of the lake to splash in the shallow water. She hoped the cool water would wash away all her hot, bothersome feelings.

It didn't. If anything, the afternoon closed in on the picnickers. The breeze went still and the temperature rose even higher. The heat was like a heavy blanket crushing them. There was no energy for frolicking; it was too hot to play. Some grown-ups dozed. Others were irritable, complaining about the heat. Ella heard some people actually wishing for rain, anything to cool the prairie down.

The only relief came from the water. Those with any energy left at all were either in it or on it. Ella spied little Leonard in the middle of the lake doing just what he'd promised, swimming bravely towards the far side. Bruce and Philip paddled their canoe. Handsome young men and women, much older than Ella's classmates, clustered around the boathouse getting ready to climb into canoes and rowboats. Ella saw Douglas watching the confident young men with envy. He didn't appear to be quite so grown up compared to them. Ella found she didn't really want to talk to him. All she could think of was Billy. It always came back to Billy. She sat to her waist in the shallow water, trying to cool down, her thoughts as heavy as the blanket of heat.

Billy could *not* be a thief.

In her mind's eye, she could see him standing in the middle of the wheat field sharing his wonder at the vast prairie. That boy couldn't be a thief. Ella knew it in her heart. She was absolutely sure. But what to do about it? Go back to being secret friends? Or try to clear his name?

She had to convince her father. He was the only one who could help. As quickly as she could, Ella went to the bathhouse where she had left her clothes and changed out of her bathing costume. She had to go home. She had to make her father understand.

CHAPTER 8

Tornado!

Eighteen kilometres southwest of the city a cloud appeared. Then another. The clouds grew dark. They moved across the sky, closer and closer to one another. With a flash of lightning, they collided. The two dark clouds – now one – began to spin, slowly at first, then faster and faster. The sky all around turned an eerie and unnatural green.

South of the city a homesteader named Thomas Beare looked up. *Was it rain at last?*

As he watched, the bottom dropped out of the cloud. A searching finger of swirling air, bright white and shining, reached down to the earth. Mrs. Beare joined her husband in the yard, her eyes wide with wonder.

In seconds, the finger touched the ground and turned into a monster. It roared into their yard. Everything within its reach was sucked into the spinning funnel cloud and crushed to dust. Buildings, trees and fences disappeared. They ran for their lives.

Across the road Walter Stephenson's farm was next. The funnel sucked his house from over him and smashed it into toothpicks. It sucked Walter up too, then threw him back into the broken remains of the house. It hurled his young wife across the farmyard. It stole the shoes off her feet. But they survived.

Nearby at the Kerr farm, the tornado crushed the life from its first victim.

The shiny white funnel was now dark with dirt and wreckage. It veered north, straight towards Regina.

It was 4:50 p.m., late Sunday afternoon, July 30.

The sky over Wascana Lake darkened and a few drops of rain fell. There was a sudden flash of forked lightning. Ella looked up, startled. She saw Leonard stop swimming and tread water as he looked at the sky. Then he turned and swam for shore. That was smart. Who wanted to be in the lake during an electrical storm? Bruce and Philip weren't worried. They kept paddling their canoe. The young people in the boathouse started to close windows and doors. The wind picked up.

Ella looped the strap of her Brownie around her neck, grabbed the picnic basket and started up Smith Street. She had to hurry, or she'd get wet. As she walked, Ella went over in her head what she'd say to her father. It was going to be hard to describe how she knew Billy was innocent. Her father would want proof and she didn't have any. She felt another drop of rain. She walked faster, the empty picnic basket bumping against her legs.

Then she heard a train.

That was odd. The train tracks were north of the city, but the sound was coming from the south. How could that be? Strange as it was, the noise definitely sounded like a train and it was getter louder by the second. What was it? All she could see were dark clouds. It was going to be a fearsome storm. She ran.

The deadly funnel careened around the corner of the brand-new Legislative Building, smashing all its windows. It reached a tendril of wind inside the building that sucked out furniture, tore out walls and created a baby whirlwind out of last week's provincial examination papers. The noise was deafening.

Sucking great gulps of the lake into its vortex, the funnel became a waterspout. The spinning column of water cut straight across the lake, flinging boats and people in all directions. Bruce and Philip clutched their paddles and closed their eyes as the spout lifted them high into the air and threw them into nearby Wascana Park. Two brave young men tried to hold the boathouse door shut against the terrible wind but were sucked out of the building, the door torn from its hinges. The entire building shook itself into rubble behind them.

The funnel cloud narrowed its sights on the city. It tightened its girth to a mere 150 metres and spun faster, always counter-clockwise, until the winds were spinning at 400 kilometres an hour. Heavy with lake water, full of whirling debris, it turned slightly to cut a northeasterly path towards Smith Street, straight into the beautiful heart of the Queen City.

The rain came down faster. Ella was going to get drenched. She tucked her camera inside her blouse. As she ran down Smith Street, she saw mothers get up from porch chairs, heard them call to their children to come inside. Then Douglas raced past her.

"Ella, RUN!" he shouted.

"What?" Ella stopped in confusion. But Douglas was gone. She looked back down Smith Street and could just make out Wascana Park several blocks away. She squinted. Another figure came out of the park and ran down Smith Street. Leonard! But he wasn't running, he was flying, almost as if he were being pushed from behind. A second later, Ella could see why. A monstrous funnel cloud was following Leonard, and they were both headed straight for her.

Ella stared at the funnel cloud. Then she screamed. She couldn't stop herself. But nobody heard. The sound was stolen by the colossal wind. It inhaled the very breath from her lungs. She dropped the basket and ran for her life.

Wicked glass splinters from broken windows shot through the air like tiny daggers. A car flew into Mrs. Waddell's parlour. In her panic, Ella ran up Smith Street. But that was foolish. She couldn't outrun the cyclone; she had to get out of its way. Ella struggled to make her brain work. She veered right, turning east, away from Smith Street. She ran across Lorne Street, then Cornwall Street, all the way to Scarth. The roar of the wind was all around her and she couldn't tell where the cyclone was any more, so she risked a glance over her shoulder. She saw a man being chased by a barrel. She saw the top floor of William Beelby's home lift off and land in his neighbour's front yard. But she was farther away from the deadly funnel than before. It was still moving north. Ella kept running east.

The tornado shifted slightly east, pausing at Victoria Park. Some trees in the park were stripped of their bark, then pulled out of the soil and peeled like bananas. Others were left untouched. The fountain blew apart, just as a husband and wife out walking were picked up and hurled into the library. Whole sections of the library, the church and the YMCA crumbled under the force of the wind. The thousands of tiny electric lights that had just been strung disappeared. The tornado tore the roof off the Telephone Exchange building and caved in one wall. The fifteen-ton switchboard on the top floor crashed down into the basement, carrying the telephone operators with it.

The school was just ahead, but the door was locked. It had a basement, where Miss Hayward stored extra desks and chairs. Ella kicked open the basement window and crawled inside. Her ears were popping and her head felt like it was going to explode. She hid under one of the old desks, put her hands over her ears and tried to stop shaking.

The wind pushed north to the Warehouse District. Boxcars hurtled through the air above the rail yards, smashing into one another. Sturdy brick warehouses were crushed. Jock's wooden house disappeared as the top floor of the Ackerman Building fell on top of it. And his wasn't the only one destroyed. Beyond the warehouses were hundreds of homes for the working men of Regina and their families. The tornado cut a path right through them.

The tornado found George Appleby. Being a scout, he knew what to do, running for shelter as fast as he could. He wasn't fast enough. Just as he reached a nearby building, it exploded from the inside and a wall fell on top of him. He was the tornado's last victim.

As the tornado headed north out of Regina, the giant funnel added one last insult. It dumped all the remaining water it had picked up from Wascana Lake onto the city, a freezing deluge that poured through the gaping holes left in the buildings.

At 4:55 p.m. the whistle on the powerhouse blew a warning to residents. But it came too late. It had taken just five minutes to tear Regina apart.

CHAPTER 9

City in Ruins

The world had gone quiet. Ella crawled out from under the desk. *Was it over?*

She didn't want to climb back out the window so she made her way upstairs and left the school by the front door. She couldn't lock the door behind her, but she had a feeling nobody was going to care. She desperately wanted to go home, but she was scared. What if the cyclone had wrecked her house? What if her parents were hurt? Or worse?

Ella walked slowly towards Victoria Avenue. She still felt shaky, but so far, the damage on this street wasn't too bad. Gardens were messy and windblown. Odd things were stuck in fences – a bicycle wheel, a toilet seat, a doll. In one yard a huge pile of clothes blocked the path to the house. Clotheslines were wrapped around trees. Ella stopped to snap a photo. She was glad she had her Brownie with her. This was definitely a story.

Ella was nearly to her block. She closed her eyes as she turned the corner. Did she dare look? Ella opened her eyes and sighed in relief. There was no car stuck in their parlour. Their top floor wasn't in somebody else's yard. Her house was just fine. Ella bounded up the porch steps and yanked open the screen door.

"Daddy!" she cried "Mother!"

"Ella!" cried Mrs. Barclay. "I'm so glad you're home. The storm arrived so suddenly and I was worried about all you children down at the lake. Did you get wet?"

Ella looked at her mother in disbelief. "Wet?"

"And that wind," her mother went on. "The noisiest I've ever heard. It blew some clothes right off our clothesline! There may well be some damage in town. We don't usually get wind like that."

She didn't know. The storm had hit only a block away but she didn't know.

Ella burst into tears.

Mrs. Barclay, surprised, put her arms around her daughter and held her tight. "Ella, what's wrong? Are you cold?" she asked. "I can make you a cup of tea."

"No, Mother, no!" said Ella. "It's just...it wasn't an ordinary storm. I had to run and run and I had to break into the school and...and..." Ella was still crying and starting to hiccup.

"Mr. Barclay! Mr. Isbister!"

"What on earth?" Mr. Barclay called out as he emerged from his study. Jesper followed close behind. "Why are you shouting?"

"Oh, Daddy!" Ella was in tears again. "You have to come and see!"

Ella dragged her father by the hand to the porch and down into the street. She pointed towards Victoria Park. "Look!"

As her family looked about in shock, Ella snapped a picture. She could see in her mind's eye what the photo would look like. It would look like the end of the world.

"See, Daddy? It was a cyclone!"

Dazed, they all walked down the road. Victoria Park was a wreck. Knox Presbyterian Church, built of stone and meant to last forever, was gutted. The interior was gone, the great stained glass windows lying in pieces on the ground. A wall was gone, torn apart stone by stone, and two turrets were missing. Outside, one of the trees around the church had been stripped bare of leaves and bark, but the others looked perfectly all right. How could that be?

"This was no cyclone," Mr. Barclay said, shaking his head.

"They don't cause this much damage. It was a tornado, Ella. Much, much worse than a cyclone."

The YMCA was missing its roof and most of the outside walls around the top floor. Ella could see right into the upper dormitories. She angled her camera up and pushed the button. What had happened to the people who lived in those rooms?

The beautiful red brick Methodist Church was destroyed. It used to have a huge square tower that reached nearly five storeys into the air but only three storeys were left, and only one wall of the rest of the building. Around it was a sea of crushed brick and splintered lumber. The church had been completed just eighteen months earlier.

With that much damage done to the mighty, most substantial buildings in Regina, what chance was there for ordinary family homes?

"Isbister!" cried Mr. Barclay. "We need to go back and get some shovels. Alex! We'll need bandages. Lots of them."

Alex? Only in a catastrophe would her father use her mother's Christian name.

Mrs. Barclay grabbed Ella's hand. "Come. We must do as your father says. Help me pack a first aid kit. There will be people hurt." Ella and her mother rushed home to tear sheets into strips. Mr. Barclay and Jesper were close behind to collect shovels from the cellar. At the last minute, Ella grabbed more film for her Brownie and stuffed it in her pocket. They hurried back outside.

Bewildered people stumbled from buildings. The scene was so overwhelming, so impossible, it was hard to believe it was true. Ella snapped another photo.

Wooden houses lay crushed into useless piles of lumber or leaned drunkenly off their foundations. As Ella watched, one house leaned further, further, further, until with a crack of snapped beams, the whole house fell on its side. She caught her breath. There didn't seem to be any windows left in any of the houses, and few roofs. Brick houses had not been spared. Whole floors were blown to who knew where, porches and balconies torn away, walls collapsed. Cries and shouts and moans came from all directions. With two shovels and some torn sheets, what could they do?

At the Guthrie Cottage on Lorne Street, a young man sat dazed on top of a pile of rubble. All around him men were digging. The Barclays headed that way. One of the diggers spoke to Mr. Barclay.

"Six people lived in that house. He's the only one got out," said the man quietly. "He's not much use now." Ella didn't think the young man looked hurt but he was shaking. She looked more closely. He cradled a diamond engagement ring in his hands. As she watched, he shook so hard he dropped the precious ring. It fell into a heap of splintered wood but the young man didn't seem to notice.

An ambulance sped around the corner, stopping at Joseph Jack's rooming house. Three people were carried out and there was a cloth over the face of one of them. Ella had never seen a dead body before. She didn't want to know who it was.

Outside the next house, Mr. Loggie was comforting his wife. Their house looked odd, as if it had burst open from the inside, exploded almost. The doors and windows weren't broken. They were shredded. Mrs. Loggie bent over a tiny bundle in her arms, weeping as if she would never stop. Mrs. Barclay rushed to Mrs. Loggie and put her arms around her. Ella followed, wanting to help. She reached out to take the baby but Mrs. Loggie wouldn't let him go. The blanket dropped from his tiny face and Ella saw that he was dead. The pressure of the explosion had been too much for him. She stepped back in horror.

Ella backed into the street. She didn't know where to look or what to do, so she sank down on the curb, shut her eyes and hugged her knees. That baby was dead. It was so, so awful. Two big tears rolled down her cheeks. Never in her whole entire life had she imagined that anything this terrible could happen where she lived. Ella put her head down on her knees and sobbed.

"Are you hurt?"

Ella felt a tap on her shoulder. She lifted her face and looked into the worried face of a stranger.

"I'm fine," she stammered. "Don't worry about me."

The stranger moved off. Ella dried her face on her sleeve, just as if she were a boy. What good were manners now? Her mother was still comforting Mrs. Loggie. Ella quickly looked away and was amazed at what she saw in the opposite direction.

She remembered the photo she had taken of the lovely homes on Smith Street, the one her father said had good perspective. She was pretty much sitting in the same spot as the one from which she'd taken the first snapshot. Everything in that photo was gone. None of the houses were even recognizable. Ella looked down at her Brownie: *Photograph the thing that is unusual – the thing that doesn't fit*. That would be everything, thought Ella grimly. Carefully, she put in one of the new rolls of film she'd grabbed as she'd left the house and snapped a picture. Before and after. That really told a story.

Then she heard Douglas cry out. Just down the road was the Hindson home. The storm had crumbled the house and buried the whole family, all but Douglas who'd just been racing in the front door as the tornado struck.

Douglas was horribly cut and bruised, and bleeding from one ear. With their bare hands, he and a neighbour scrabbled in the rubble, pulling away timber after timber.

"I'm coming, Dad! I'm coming!" he screamed, tears rolling down his dirty face. "Hang on!"

Ella knew Douglas came from a big family. How many were under there? She couldn't bear to think. Mr. Barclay ran from the Loggie house with his shovel and began to help. Ella took her bandages to Douglas and tried to get him to tend to his ear, but he wouldn't stop. She got out of his way. It was all she could do.

Ella found it was easier to watch what was happening if she

watched through the tiny lens of the camera. Somehow, what was going on didn't seem so real that way. She took a picture of Douglas's house.

More men joined the search. Ella could hear cries coming from under the rubble. It was the worst thing she had heard in her entire life.

"Careful!" shouted her father. "If we move that beam we might kill them!" Ella felt sick. Progress was slow. More men came. Somebody brought a horse and harnessed it to one of the house's main timbers.

"Slowly, slowly!" The horse moved forward, step by step. The timber shifted. "STOP!"

Her father, Douglas and the neighbour crawled into the wreckage.

"Bring a blanket! We need more men!"

More men came. As Ella watched, the volunteers carefully lifted Douglas's father and older brother Fred from the rubble. Their arms were wrapped around one another. Neither was moving. Douglas wept and didn't care who saw.

"There's no more room at the hospital," called out a passerby. "Take the injured to the Roman Catholic Bishop's Palace! It's damaged, but usable."

Just then Ella saw Hong and Li. Their faces were masks of sorrow. She slowly walked towards them.

"Hong? Are you all right?"

Hong turned to her. "Bad, bad. Cousin Ywe, there." He pointed to the remains of Mack Lee's Chinese laundry. "Dead. No can touch. Bad spirit." A tear rolled down his face. "Ywe good man."

"He's not dead!" cried a man wearing a well-cut suit. "Come on, men, let's get him out!" A rescue squad of passersby immediately formed to dig the Chinese man out.

Hong and Li would not budge. Ywe was dead and touching the dead was not allowed. The men got Ywe out anyway, but it didn't matter. He was truly dead.

News came that some telephone operators were trapped under the fifteen-ton switchboard. A group of people rushed to the Telephone Exchange Building. Ella knew she couldn't help there. What *could* she do?

Just then she saw Mr. Beelby climbing through a broken window. He looked astonished to see the top floor of his house sitting in the neighbour's yard. Carefully he helped his wife through the window. She stood shakily, her hands jerking convulsively.

"Where is she?" Mrs. Beelby cried in anguish. "Where is

my baby? Where is my little girl?" Ella couldn't bear to think another child had been killed. She rushed over to Mrs. Beelby.

"I'll help you find her," she said breathlessly. "How old is your baby? What's her name?"

"Florence," sobbed Mrs. Beelby. "She's three years old." Ella looked around. Where to start? The street was such a jumble of junk. There were chairs and tables scattered everywhere, even a stove sitting in the middle of the road. Ella tried the neighbour's yard first. That's where the top floor of the Beelby house was sitting. Maybe Florence was nearby? But no, Ella couldn't see her anywhere.

"Florence?" she called out. "Where are you, Florence?"

Ella heard a whimper and tried to follow it to its source. It seemed to be coming from the street. Ella looked under bushes, behind crushed buggies, under porches. A three-year-old could fit anywhere! She listened hard and heard the sound again. It came from the stove in the middle of the road.

Ella rushed over and there was little Florence Beelby. Whimpering and unbelievably dirty, but quite all right. Ella picked her up. "I guess you didn't like the rain," she said gently. "So you found your own shelter!"

Mrs. Beelby screamed when she saw Florence, grabbing her out of Ella's hands and smothering her with kisses.

Ella felt a little better now that she'd done at least one small thing to help. She couldn't dig people out and she wasn't much of a nurse. Her parents were busy. And she didn't know where Jesper had got to. Perhaps he'd gone to get the Cadillac, so he could transport people to shelters. Blankets were being used to hoist the bent and broken bodies into the backs of buggies, drays, private automobiles, anything. There were so many bodies.

There had to be something useful she could do.

Ella continued down the road. She saw so many strange things. A piano sat, nice as you please, in the middle of the road. When she came close, she saw that all the innards of the instrument had been stripped out and blown away. But there wasn't a scratch on the cabinet. A bookcase lay in the middle of someone's lawn. The wind had torn all the shelves out, except the middle one. A lady sat on a windowsill, looking out at her porch chairs. The chairs still sat on the porch, even though much of her house was gone. Ella couldn't believe the strangeness of it all. She reached for her Brownie and snapped another picture.

Mrs. Waddell stood in the middle of the road, shaking her head at the mess of her parlour. The car that had flown into it had missed her by inches. "By inches!" she exclaimed, as if she had to convince somebody. Further down the road Ella saw the little white dog, the one that wouldn't sit still for a picture. It sat quietly beside the porch of Hodsman's rooming house. The house and the porch were completely crushed.

"C'mon, you," said Ella, dangling her fingers trying to distract the dog. "Why don't we find your master?" But the dog wouldn't budge from the pile of rubble.

Ella wandered further. It was like a nightmare in daytime. She couldn't believe her beautiful city was no more. All of a sudden, a disreputable-looking old man came rushing down the road straight for her. It was Mr. Leatherby!

"Did you take it?" he demanded of Ella, waving his walking stick in her face. "Did you?"

"Take what?" asked Ella nervously.

"My turret, you silly girl! My turret's gone!"

Ella looked towards the corner. The Turret House wasn't gone, but the turret was badly damaged. Ella half smiled at the idea that only a tornado could force the old hermit to go outside.

"No, Mr. Leatherby. The wind took your turret. It was a tornado. Part of the house blew away, but nobody took it."

"Bring it back," demanded the old man. "Now!"

"Mr. Leatherby," Ella said kindly, "I'll take you to some people who can look after you until your house is fixed." She remembered that the Bishop's Palace was being used as a shelter. Mr. Leatherby didn't seem to be hurt, but he certainly needed help. There was a vagueness in his eyes that was worrying. Was he in shock? Or was his mind failing? She wondered if anybody knew that Mr. Leatherby wasn't quite right in the head any more. No wonder his family had sent Billy to look after him.

Billy.

In all the commotion, the trousers and the socks and the money and everything else had flown right out of her mind. Why wasn't Billy looking after his uncle?

"Mr. Leatherby, where's Billy? Is he hurt?" asked Ella urgently.

"Billy? Billy? Who's Billy?" mumbled the old man.

"Your nephew, Mr. Leatherby, from England," replied Ella. "The one who's staying with you."

"Nobody stays with me!" Mr. Leatherby shouted angrily. "Never!" Ella looked at him in surprise.

"Are you sure?" she asked in confusion.

"I'd know, wouldn't I?" growled Mr. Leatherby. "I'd know if some snivelling boy was messing with my stuff." Ella looked into Mr. Leatherby's eyes. Now they were sharp and bright.

"And I don't even have a nephew. Probably because I haven't got any brothers or sisters!" The old man hooted with laughter. Then his eyes clouded over, going vague once more.

"Maybe he stole my turret," he mumbled. "Make him give it back!"

Ella said no more. When they got to Bishop's Palace, she handed Mr. Leatherby into the care of the volunteers. Everything was suddenly clear. Ella kicked herself for not guessing sooner. As a liar, it was turning out that Billy wasn't a very good one. She knew exactly where she had to go to find Billy, and she had to go herself. Nobody else would know where to look.

CHAPTER 10

A Pile of Bones

There was confusion everywhere. The downtown streets were full of dazed wanderers, many bashed and bloody, shambling from one pile of rubble to another, calling out for loved ones. The air was filled with shouts and cries and moans. The phone lines were down and the switchboard crushed. The telegraph lines were gone too. Power was out throughout the city. The tornado had passed through so quickly that Reginans outside of the wind zone didn't yet know of the disaster that had struck their city.

But others, far away, did.

The telegraph wires had broken near the freight yards. As trainmen frantically pulled apart the wreckage looking for their fellow workers, they also found the broken line and snaked it up and over, under and around the crushed train cars and smashed sheds. Once free, the wire was reattached. It was 6:00 p.m. Only an hour had passed since the tragedy when a message was flashed worldwide: "Cyclone hit Regina. City in ruins."

Ella rushed back up Lorne Street. She couldn't make sense of what she was seeing. This couldn't be her beautiful city. Quickly, hardly breaking her urgent stride, she took snapshots of the lovely buildings she had once admired: the library, the park, the churches, even her father's bank. She was glad she'd thought to bring more film. She needed it all.

At the YMCA a number of young men were milling about. "Did you see that?" they kept asking one another. "I was just snoozing on my bunk on the third floor. It was so darn hot. Then that wind came! I raced down the stairs, and now look. My room is gone!" Ella closed her eyes in relief for just a moment. At least some people from the third floor dormitories had escaped.

She stopped short when she got to the Telephone Exchange. Or at least, the place where it used to be. She wouldn't have recognized the corner had it not been for the dozens of people clustered around it, discussing equipment. The building was completely gone, save for one corner that stood like an accusing finger pointing to the sky. The heavy metalwork that Ella guessed must have been the switchboard was twisted and mangled.

"We'll need jack screws to raise the beams," said one man, considering the wreckage. "Only way to get 'em out."

Get them out?! Ella put her hands over her mouth. There couldn't be people under that, could there? But there were. Ten young women, all buried. Another man said it was lucky there weren't more, it being Sunday and all. Nothing about this felt lucky to Ella. She rushed on, tears blurring her sight.

One block further north, Ella ran into the train tracks. She could see right across the railyards to the Warehouse District on the other side because everything before her was flattened to the ground. The grain elevator was gone, the roundhouse gutted. The only things that rose to any height were the railway cars lying in great piles here and there, as if a small child had thrown wooden blocks down from a great height. The Brownie recorded it all.

She wouldn't need to go all the way to Albert Street to cross the tracks. She could cross anywhere now. Carefully Ella began to pick her way through the debris. She could see the Ackerman Building straight ahead. It was damaged, but still standing. But what of the little house next door?

Regina was the headquarters of the Royal Northwest Mounted Police. The moment the storm passed, Police Officer Banting at the Regina picket tried to reach the police barracks outside of town by telephone. But with the lines down, he couldn't reach anyone. Did the others know? Had they seen the monstrous funnel cloud? Were they already on their way? Or had it hit them too? Whatever the answer, Officer Banting knew he needed to get help. So he saddled his horse and raced through town, guiding the poor animal around the rubble, leaping over piles of lumber, dodging wagons and buggies and trying his best not to kill them both.

When he arrived at the barracks, he saw men looking curiously towards town.

"That was some storm," commented one of the police officers. "We tried to call you, but it must have taken out the telephone lines."

"Cyclone!" replied Banting breathlessly as he slid off his panting horse. "It was a cyclone! The town's been flattened!"

Wide-eyed, the officers leapt out of their chairs. "Flattened? So the storm touched down? It must have been a tornado, then. How bad is the damage? Are there wounded?"

"Bad. Yes. Lots of wounded, don't know how many. Dead too. We need help!"

All 150 officers at the barracks were mobilized immediately. Orders were barked. First aid kits assembled. Horses saddled. And the Royal Northwest Mounted Police were off and running.

By the time the outside world was told of the disaster, the Mounted Police were in the city. They arrived to find hundreds of people, hats and coats off, fine suits filthy, tearing bricks and stones up with their bare hands, desperately trying to reach the people trapped beneath. There were lots of able-bodied people willing to help, but what to do first? How to do it? Where to do it?

Mayor McAra and City Commissioner Thornton met with police at city hall. They made a list. Teams of rescuers had to be sent to look for survivors; temporary hospitals set up; the wounded tended and the dead respectfully treated. Streets had to be cleared; traffic directed; shelter organized for the thousands left without homes. The lost and missing had to be accounted for; lists drawn up; family members comforted. Food and water had to be found. The telephone system had to be fixed and electricity restored. And it all had to be done right away. It was clear more men were needed to put the plan into action. The Mayor passed the word through the broken streets that one hundred good men were required immediately at City Hall. They would become "Special Constables" to help organize the rescue.

A thousand men showed up.

Maybe she should have tried Albert Street. It was so hard crawling over the rubble strewn across the tracks. But Ella kept the Ackerman Building in her sights. She tried to remember the picture she had taken of it the day she met Jock.

How much of the building was damaged? At first she'd thought just the front corner of the roof had collapsed. Now it was clear. The front corner had indeed collapsed. But it was the corner of the *fourth* floor. The fifth floor was completely gone. And Jock's little shack next door was a pile of rubble. Not a single fragment was left standing.

Was Jock inside? Was Billy?

Ella climbed over the last pile of shattered timber and ran across Dewdney Avenue. Where was everybody? Compared to the city, where hundreds of people seemed to be milling about, there was hardly a soul in the Warehouse District.

"Billy! Billy!" cried Ella as loudly as she could. "Where are you? Billy Forsythe, YOU ANSWER ME!"

Ella saw a four-foot length of timber fly into the air, followed by a small avalanche of rubble that rolled down the edge of the pile of splintered wood that used to be Jock's home. A head popped up. It was Billy!

"Ella! Ella! You've got to help me! Jock's trapped!"

By seven o'clock teams had fanned out through the city led by police officers, city aldermen and special constables. By 7:15, a special train had arrived from nearby Moose Jaw carrying doctors and nurses. Teams of buggies took the volunteers to the various makeshift hospitals set up throughout the city. A call went out for electricians to go to Moore's Light Company. Mr. Moore had placed the full facilities of his factory in the hands of the city to help get the power back on. The race was on.

And it was indeed a race. The sun was setting.

Desperately, Ella and Billy tried to move the debris all by themselves. But it was too heavy, and there was just too much. At first, Ella had been able to hear Jock's weak cries coming from beneath the pile. She couldn't hear him anymore. She remembered his lusty voice singing "Oh bury me not on the lone prairie." She couldn't let him die.

"This isn't working, Billy," she said urgently. "We have to get help!"

"Nobody will help us," replied Billy angrily. "Do you see anybody around? We're nothing. They won't come."

Ella wasn't sure if it was what Billy said or the fact that it might be true that made her more upset. She couldn't let it be true.

"No," she said firmly. "They'll come. Keep talking to him." And Ella raced off. She needed to find someone – anyone – or Jock would die. She ran down Dewdney Avenue, shouting at the top of her lungs.

"Help! Help! We need help!"

Ella stuck her head in doorways, opened tavern doors, peered into every shadow and rushed down every dark alley. She wasn't afraid. What was the point of being afraid of what might happen when something far worse already had? She pleaded and begged and shouted in a very unladylike fashion, and she didn't stop until she had what she wanted. By the time she got back to the Ackerman Building, she had a team of twelve burly men with her, all armed with shovels.

Someone handed Ella a lantern. "Hold it steady," said a voice. The men poked and prodded with their shovels. "Careful, now."

It had become so dark. They'd been working for a long time, but still the men had not been able to release Jock from his prison. It wasn't the remains of his house that were the problem, it was the roof of the Ackerman Building that had fallen on top of it. Levers were needed to tip the heavy beams off the rubble. After a single grateful glance at Ella when she arrived with help, Billy had continued to work frantically. Now he was nearly beside himself. One of the men put his arm around the boy.

"Give yourself a break, son," he said kindly. "We won't give up till we find your friend." The man went back to digging. Billy rocked back on his haunches, exhausted.

"Billy, over here," called Ella softly. "There's water in the jug." Billy took a slug right from the big jug. Water splashed over his face, creating rivulets of mud that ran down his cheeks and neck, right down under his shirt. Ella wanted to laugh at the sight, but couldn't. None of this was funny. Billy pulled his filthy shirt off and wiped his face. It didn't help. In the dark, Ella could see the sweat shine on his body. He'd worked so hard. They *had* to save Jock.

"Why'd you come, Ella? Why'd you come *here?*"

"Because I know you don't live in the Turret House. It was the only other place I could think of. He's your father, isn't he?" asked Ella quietly. "And you fell on hard times. So you made up that story about your mam and your brothers back in England."

"No," said Billy shortly. "You're wrong. You don't know nuthin'. Why wouldn't you talk wi' me last week?"

Now it was Ella's turn to feel uncomfortable. "I couldn't. When I got home, I got in trouble. My father said I couldn't talk to you ever again."

"Because I'm poor. Because I'm not educated. Because I'm not good enough for the likes of you," he said bitterly.

That made Ella's blood boil. "No! It's because you're a thief!" She almost dropped the lantern, she was so angry. "There, I've said it. I didn't want to believe it when my father told me, because the Billy I thought I knew wouldn't do anything like that! I didn't want to accuse you. But all you ever do is tell lies, so what am I supposed to think? I believed my parents because I couldn't believe you!"

Billy stared at Ella in shock. Finally he said quietly, "It's not a story about me mam, or me bruvvers." He sighed. "I wish Jock was my father. It feels like 'e should be." Billy was so tired his carefully practiced speech was slipping. He looked wryly at Ella. "When you're goin' to tell a whopper, best be that you stick as close to the truth as you can."

"So, what is the truth, Billy Forsythe? You've got to tell, because people are saying bad things about you. You're in trouble. How can anybody tell what part's truth and what part's lies when it's all mixed together?" Ella was so frustrated with him that it was hard to keep her voice quiet. "Own up, Billy Forsythe, or I won't ever be your friend."

"Eureka!" There was a great shout from the men. Billy hopped up and ran to where they were gathered.

"Girl, bring the light here!" Ella hurried over with the lantern.

The men had created a small tunnel in the debris. "Boy, you're the smallest. Can you wriggle down there?" Billy wasted no time. His skinny arm snaked down into the hole, then his shoulder. He wriggled deeper and deeper until he was mostly in the hole himself. He closed his eyes and all could see the strain on his face as he reached and reached. Finally, there was a whoop of success.

"I've got his hand! And he squeezed it!" A cheer went up. Ever so gently the men worked at widening the hole. Billy kept hold of Jock's hand, and twisted his body all around to make a path. Finally the area had been opened up enough for Jock to come sliding through. The men helped Billy out of the way, but he didn't leave Jock until he'd given his hand one last big squeeze.

"This is it, Jock!" he cried. "You're coming out!"

With Billy out of the way, the strongest of the men put their arms down the hole and slowly, carefully, dragged the old man out into the open air. Jock wheezed. The men rolled him over, quick as anything, and pounded him on the back to help him get rid of all the dirt and dust that had settled in his nose and throat. Ella turned her back. All that spitting was disgusting. For a moment, she thought it was her mother thinking those words. But she thought it was disgusting too. When the hacking and hawking was done, Ella turned around again. And her heart sank. Jock was covered in blood, his arms and legs bent at impossible angles.

The men lifted him carefully onto a blanket and put him in the back of a waiting dray. The horse pranced restlessly. It could smell the blood. *Please Jock, don't die!*

Billy hopped onto the front seat of the dray. "I'm staying wi' him," he called out. "Thank you!" It wasn't until she watched the dray head off towards the Grey Nuns Hospital that Ella realized he still hadn't told her his story.

And that she was all alone in the Warehouse District past dark.

All of a sudden there was a shout nearby. "It's George! George Appleby! Come quick!"

The lantern was grabbed from Ella's hand and the men ran in the direction of the shouts. Ella didn't follow. She was left alone in utter darkness. All the shouts and screams and moans of the last few hours crowded into her head. The shadows and the alleys once again became fearsome places. This was not her city, maimed and broken, struggling to survive. Her city was the Queen City. The beautiful city. She wanted it back.

Her courage was completely spent. All the sights and sounds and smells of the past few hours caught up with her. She started to shake and had to wrap her arms around herself to control the trembling. Looking all around, jumping at shadows, Ella forced herself to take a step towards Albert Street and people. Towards home.

Word of the disaster spread throughout the city. More and more volunteers poured in bringing what supplies and skills they could offer. Rumours spread as well. Stories of hundreds dead at Wascana Lake and fires raging throughout the city. As dark fell, crews of rescuers were forced to stop work and the devastated citizens of Regina were led to the homes of neighbours, the ones who still had homes, to be bedded down for the night. Throughout the city the only sound that could be heard was the haunting call of a bugle playing "The Last Post." *It echoed throughout the silent city, a death knell for the Queen City now reduced to its namesake, a pile of bones.*

CHAPTER 11

Dominion Day

July 1st dawned clear and sunny. There were no celebrations. The strings of lights were broken, the bunting ripped to shreds. As were the lives of those left behind by the tornado. Any flags left flew at half-mast.

The city awoke, bruised and tattered. Exhausted men with blistered hands went back to work with a will, digging under the rubble for survivors. Others turned their minds to the future – to cleaning up and rebuilding. But those were tasks so immense that it was difficult to know where to start, especially when there was still grieving to be done.

"Ella! Get up immediately!" Her mother called from the hall.

Ella groaned. She didn't think she could move. Her body ached in places she hadn't known even existed. She was scraped and scratched everywhere, and under the scratches she could feel the bruises deep under her skin. Her nails were broken and chipped and her hair felt like a rat's nest. Slowly, Ella eased first one foot then the other onto the floor. She looked at the pile of clothes she'd dumped in the corner late the night before. Ruined. She stood, looking down at her soft silk nightdress. It was spotted with blood from her cuts and slivers. She yanked it off over her head and stood in front of the mirror.

She looked terrible. Last night had been bad enough. Sneaking in hadn't worked, not with both her parents waiting for her at the door, her mother crazy with worry.

"Get to bed, young lady, and we'll deal with this in the morning!" Mr. Barclay had raged, while Jesper lounged in the corner smiling his infuriating smile.

Ella had been so tired she'd simply bowed her head and let the shouting roll over her. But now it was morning. Her battered appearance was not going to help anything. The bruises blossoming all over her body were proof of what she'd done. She didn't even have the excuse that the tornado had done it; she'd done it to herself. Ella sighed. No point putting it off. Slowly, painfully, she got dressed and eased her way down the stairs to the breakfast room. She slid into her seat, grimacing when she heard her mother's gasp of horror.

"Ella, what have you done to yourself?"

Ella sighed. There was no making this story pretty. And she was tired of lying.

"I went to the Warehouse District to find Billy."

There was stunned silence around the table. Even Jesper wiped the smirk off his face.

"You did WHAT?" bellowed her father.

Ella took a deep breath. "Daddy, you're wrong about Billy."

"How dare you!"

Ella cringed. "Daddy, please don't be angry. You told me to look for the story, to see the things in the background. It all tells me that everyone is wrong about Billy. Even so, I wasn't thinking about him after the tornado. Not until I talked to Mr.

Leatherby. He gave me proof, Daddy, that Billy was a liar. But not a thief. And I was worried. Where was he? I knew of only one other place he could be if he wasn't at the Turret House, and that was the Warehouse District."

Ella took a deep breath. Both her parents looked furious, but at least they were listening. "I also knew that nobody else would look for him. I *had* to go. When I got there, Billy was trying to move a house all by himself. His friend Jock was buried underneath. I tried to help, but even together we couldn't do it. I told Billy we needed help. He said nobody would come, that he was poor, that he was nothing, and nobody would ever help him. I couldn't let that be true. So I found some men. They did come, and they helped. It got dark so I had to hold the lantern." Ella paused for a moment.

"We got Jock out. But he was just barely alive." Ella squeezed her eyes shut to stop seeing the images of his broken body. Then she added simply, "After that, I came home." She didn't tell them how frightened she'd been, how much she'd wanted her mother, how foolish she'd felt to have gone all alone. They didn't need to know.

No one said anything.

Finally, Mr. Barclay shook his head. "Have you any idea how much worry you caused, Ella? Your mother was sick with it. It was beyond inconsiderate to add an unnecessary worry at a time when we have so many real worries."

"Yes, Daddy," replied Ella quietly. "But Jock would have died."

"Ella, it was not your concern!" said Mrs. Barclay angrily. "There are many things a young lady can do at a time like this that do not involve wandering around the Warehouse District at night!"

"Yes, Mother," sighed Ella. "I'm truly sorry." And she was. But she'd do it again if she had to. What was more important than saving a man's life?

"Just so we're absolutely clear, Ella, Billy and his friend are no longer your concern. And since I can no longer trust that you will do as you're told, you may not leave your mother's side from this point forward. Mrs. Barclay, perhaps you have a more suitable job for Ella today? One that does not require a lantern or a trip to the Warehouse District?" he added sarcastically. Ella hung her head.

"I certainly do," replied Mrs. Barclay. "While you were gallivanting around the Warehouse District last night, the IODE met at Mrs. Duncan's home. We formed committees to organize shelter for the homeless and collect clothing and food. The Black Block is being turned into an operational headquarters for the volunteers. You will come with me, Ella. You will sit at a desk and you will make lists and you will add figures and you will not move from your spot until I bring you home. Do you understand?"

"Yes, Mother." Ella couldn't imagine anything more boring than lists when the whole city was in such a mess. She wanted to be outside, be a part of it all. And she hadn't been "gallivanting," she thought indignantly, but trying to save the life of a friend! But today was definitely not the day to argue.

Mr. Barclay pushed his plate away and got up from the table. "Isbister and I will be at the bank. I've been asked to coordinate the subscription list. Ladies, be ready to go in half an hour and I will walk with you."

After breakfast, Mrs. Barclay put soothing ointment on Ella's scratches and scrapes, shaking her head the whole while. "You're a mess!" she exclaimed again.

"I'm sorry, Mother," Ella apologized again.

"At least you have an exciting story to go with those scrapes," said her mother, flashing a quick smile. For that brief moment, Alex was back. Ella gave her mother a big hug. "I was afraid without you last night, Mother. I was so afraid!" she blurted out. Mrs. Barclay held her tight.

"There is no courage without fear, my sweet girl," she murmured.

In exactly one half hour the family met at the front door. Mr. Barclay was dressed as he always was for work, with his fine suit, clean white shirt and neatly tied cravat. So was Jesper. Their clothes looked out of place today. Ella took her father's hand as they walked down the street.

"What's a subscription list, Daddy?"

"It's a list of donations, Ella. Look around," he pointed behind them, to the damaged side of Victoria Park. "Do you think we should fix all those damaged buildings?"

"Of course, Daddy! Why wouldn't we?" said Ella in confusion.

"Because it will cost a great deal of money, for lumber and bricks and carpenters and electricians and painters. Who do you think should pay?"

"The people who own the buildings, maybe?"

"That's a good idea. But is it fair? The tornado was nobody's fault. At our house all we have to do is replace some missing laundry. I can afford to do that. But what of those who lost their whole house? What if they can't afford it? Should they be forced to live in the street?" questioned Mr. Barclay.

"No, that wouldn't be right," mused Ella. "Does the bank have enough money to fix everything?"

At this, Jesper laughed. Ella glared at him.

"No, even the bank doesn't have enough money for all this, Ella." Her father smiled.

"How about the city?" asked Ella. "The city has money."

"Again, not enough," replied her father.

Ella was stymied. "I can't think of anything else, Daddy. What will we do?" she asked in some panic. Not rebuild the beautiful city? That would be terrible!

"We make a subscription list, Ella. We will be able to rebuild the city if everyone works together. We hope that lots and lots of people, not just from Regina but from all over, will hear of our trouble and want to help. Many will send money, a little bit here and a little bit there. My bank will put the money in a safe place and if we put it all together, we can rebuild the city. What do you think about that, Ella?"

"I think it's grand, Daddy, but will people from far away care about our trouble?"

"We'll see, Ella. We'll see."

They reached the Black Block. Mrs. Barclay marched Ella inside and sat her down at a table with a map, a scribbler and a pencil. One of the volunteers came to talk with them.

"Young lady, are you a brave girl?"

After last night, Ella could honestly say she was.

"Good then. Our most important task is to make sure that we account for all the citizens of Regina. We must find every single soul and reunite them with their family. Dead or alive," he added sadly. "As the searchers report in with information, can you keep a list?"

She nodded solemnly and picked up the pen. As her mother moved on to another task, Ella carefully created three lists in the scribbler. The first list was for the names of the living, with space for a note to tell friends and family where they were staying. The second list was for the names of the injured, noting the hospital where they were being treated. And the last list was for the names of the dead. Throughout the day, rescuers came to the Black Block to tell Ella which houses had been searched and who they found there. Ella noted the names on the correct list and put an X over the house on the map. Distraught family members came to check her lists, desperately looking for lost loved ones and praying they weren't on the list of the dead. As the day went on, the lists grew long and Xs were scrawled all over the map.

Mid-morning, there was a huge commotion at the Black Block. Ella looked up in surprise. It was a large group of doctors and nurses, just arrived by special train from Winnipeg. "Put us to work!" they said. "We've come to help."

Tears came to Ella's eyes. Her daddy was right. People from far away did care about Regina's troubles. And Billy was wrong. It didn't matter if you were rich or poor.

The Grey Nuns Hospital was a seething mass of people. The wounded were everywhere; some on stretchers, some on chairs, some on the floor. Those who could stand waited patiently for their turn to be treated as the volunteer doctors and nurses worked on those most badly hurt. Jock was one of them.

Billy held Jock's hand tightly. He would not let go. Jock was all he had, after all. And for all his brave words, Billy was smart enough to know that it didn't look good for poor Jock. He could tell that both of Jock's legs were broken, and maybe his shoulder too. His breathing wasn't good, either. Did that mean a busted rib? Or worse? And there was so much blood. What if he was hurt inside?

Billy's scrappy skills from the streets of London came in handy. He bullied the nurses and the doctors, never once letting go of Jock's hand. Billy just yelled. It was hard to say if Jock got treatment because of his terrible wounds, or to make Billy shut up. Whatever it was, by mid-morning Jock was whisked away to surgery. Reluctantly, Billy let go of Jock's hand.

Ella was distracted by the earnest Boy Scouts that haunted the Black Block throughout the day. The morning paper had put out a call to all Boy Scouts to report to the newspaper office by ten o'clock that morning. They were to be messengers, relaying needed information between the volunteers operating across the city.

"You're like a human telephone!" said Ella when James Duncan, the pharmacist's son, dropped off the morning paper to the Black Block.

"I've got to go. I'm very busy," said James proudly. "I'm looking for Bruce and Philip. They didn't report for Scout duty this morning. Did you hear? Major Embury's ordered the militia back to town! They're all coming back to help. The 95th Rifles, the 16th Mounted Rifles and the 26th Rifles – they're all coming! Do you think there might be a parade?" Ella smiled sadly at his enthusiasm as he ran off to deliver his next message.

She picked up the morning *Leader*. The headlines jumped out at her.

31 Known Dead; Over 100 Hurt in Disaster
All real men asked to help.

Women too, thought Ella as she added the figures on her lists. It was early days, yet, for tallies. She feared it might get worse, much worse. Many buildings on her map were still short an X.

Everyone who stopped in at the Black Block had a story to share. It was hard to know which ones to believe.

"Did you know there are hundreds dead at the bottom of Wascana Lake, all drowned? There are so many bodies they've decided to dynamite the lake to bring them to the surface!" said one man.

Ella dropped her pencil in horror. She thought of all her friends at the picnic. That couldn't be true! Leaving her post, she rushed to find her mother, tears beginning to fill her eyes.

"Mother!" she cried, "the picnic, they said..."

It took a while to straighten things out. Finally word came back from the police that the lake *wasn't* filled with bodies. She didn't stop shaking for a long time after that. Especially since some of the awful stories were true.

Bruce Langton hadn't reported for Scout duty because he had been found unconscious in Wascana Park, still in his canoe, still clutching his paddle. Poor Philip's name was on the list of the dead. He'd been thrown from the canoe during its wild ride atop the waterspout.

Leonard, after his run with the wind, was found exhausted by a stranger and taken to a nearby house. His name was on the list of injured.

The two young men who had tried to hold the boathouse door shut had different fates. One was tossed into Wascana Park, his feet crushed. Feeling no pain he walked on those feet all night looking for his friend. His friend was found two blocks away, dead. The doctor said it would be weeks before the grieving man could walk again.

Douglas's brother Fred had been hit with debris from behind and thrown into his father's arms, where they both tumbled down the stairs. Fred was gone, but miraculously, Mr. Hindson – and all the rest of the Hindsons – were going to be all right.

The women trapped in the Telephone Exchange all escaped with fewer scratches than Ella herself. The paper reported that one woman's back was broken and she was dying in hospital, but as that woman was currently helping out at the Black Block, Ella had been quick to assure everyone that, to the best of her knowledge, the woman was not dying. Every tragic story that turned to mirth was a gift.

It was the happiest and saddest day Ella had ever spent in her whole life. She came to know by the faces of the rescuers if they had found a body buried in the rubble. The horror lingered in their eyes. And she dreaded the hope and fear that played on the faces of those who came to check the lists. Alive or dead? Lost forever, or just for today? Women wept when they heard bad news and had to be helped away from her table. Ella thought of her mother and how she might have wept had she heard of Ella's body found in the Warehouse District. How she herself might have wept had it been her mother or father trapped and crushed. It was too terrible to think about.

Her bruises felt like nothing now. It was going to take a different kind of courage to get through this terrible day.

CHAPTER 12

Where is Billy?

Mrs. Barclay and Ella walked home together at lunchtime. Ella hadn't yet figured out how to sneak over to the Grey Nuns and find out how Jock was doing. She sighed. It felt awful to be at odds with her parents.

Hamilton Street was quiet. But as they turned onto Victoria Avenue and got closer to the storm zone, there were people everywhere. Gardeners in the park cut down damaged trees and piled up broken branches for burning. Men in overalls shovelled crushed bricks into carts to be taken away. Carpenters sawed up broken timbers. Gangs of men hurled debris out of broken homes, trying to make them somewhat habitable. Men in suits carried clipboards and took notes. Ella saw Mayor McAra sending men here, there and everywhere. The RNWMP directed traffic and helped load wagons. A crowd gathered at the church to watch as workers dug through the wreckage looking for more survivors. And everywhere Ella looked she saw photographers taking snapshots.

"Where did they all come from?" she asked her mother in wonder.

"They came on the train," replied her mother with a sniff. "Poking their noses into our business. Busybodies!"

Ella thought about that for a minute. "Maybe it's a good thing, Mother," she finally said. "Daddy told me about the subscription list. Maybe if people far away see pictures of all the damage, they'll be more willing to send money to help us."

"Hmmphh," Mrs. Barclay sniffed. Ella had to smile. It was becoming her mother's favourite word. "Charity begins at home. We can look after ourselves. We always have."

"I don't think we can this time, Mother," replied Ella sadly. "It's too much for us." Mrs. Barclay just looked grim.

Mr. Barclay and Jesper did not come home for lunch. Ella and her mother ate quickly. Remembering the photographers, Ella collected her Brownie film to take to the pharmacy on the way. They headed back to their jobs.

Ella worked on her lists throughout the afternoon, all the while wondering about Jock. Billy would still be at the hospital, but where would he sleep tonight? Ella couldn't stop worrying, even though there was plenty of distraction at the Black Block. It had become the command post for Regina's recovery. There was so much to be done. Tents had to be found for the families left homeless. Where to put them? Victoria Park was in ruins. What about mail? Whole addresses had ceased to exist. Supply depots for food and water had to be established. And messages poured into the telegraph office. Somebody had to answer them all.

From Mayor Mayberry of Moose Jaw:

Much distressed at fragmentary news of your calamity. We have no particulars but are sending some nurses on the train.

Can we do anything else?

From Mayor Waugh of Winnipeg:

Winnipeg shocked at disaster which has befallen your city and sympathizes with bereaved and sufferers. Can we do anything to assist you?

Mayor Mitchell of Calgary:

Appalled at great loss and disaster your city has experienced. City of Calgary anxious to relieve. Wire quick what is most needed; our sympathy to all sufferers.

W.E. Burke, Board of Trade, Moose Jaw:
We have 50 or 60 tents which we would be glad to ship to you by first train. If you need them wire immediately.

President of the Chicago Association of Commerce:

The Association notes with deepest sympathy your city's severe loss in life and property by cyclone. Chicago knows the influence of disaster upon people of spirit and purpose like yourself. We mourn with you over your dead and foresee with you the immediate restoration of the stricken sections of your wonderful city.

People of spirit and purpose. Yes, we are, thought Ella. *Yes, we are!* The messages filled her with hope. But they didn't get the job done. That was up to the people of Regina. Ella went back to her lists with a will. Together, they could do it.

The long day crashed down on Ella's head just before dinner. Mrs. Barclay and Ella once again walked towards home. The house was empty. Mrs. Dudek had prepared a cold supper and gone home early to her own family. Ella set the table. Her father did not come home. Ella and her mother went to the parlour and exchanged news of the day. Still Mr. Barclay did not come home. Mrs. Barclay decided that they should eat, regardless, just as the front door crashed open and Mr. Barclay strode into the parlour, closely followed by Jesper.

"Ella!" he shouted. Both Ella and her mother jumped to their feet in surprise. Mrs. Barclay put her hand to her breast as she saw her husband's angry face.

"WHERE IS BILLY FORSYTHE?"

Ella trembled. What had happened now?

"I don't know, Daddy. I haven't seen him since last night when he went to the hospital with Jock."

"Well," boomed Mr. Barclay. "He is not at the hospital now. This Jock fellow went into surgery late this morning. Billy disappeared after that. And we have discovered another theft – from the bank no less! One of our tellers was nearby right after the tornado hit and saw a skinny boy running past the bank toward the Warehouse District. He didn't take any notice of it then, but remembered once we found the theft. The teller told Isbister, who told me. The boy must have crawled through a broken window and picked the lock on our petty cash drawer, just like he picked the lock on the door of the Regina Trading Company. He was clearly taking advantage of the disaster. I told you, Ella, he is a thief and MUST be stopped!"

A theft from the bank? It was unthinkable. She felt sick inside. But she still couldn't believe it.

"Daddy, I told you Billy went to the Warehouse District after the tornado to find Jock. Just because he passed the bank doesn't mean he stole the money."

"Ella, stop this foolishness. Where can we find him? You *must* tell us."

"Truly, Daddy, I don't know!" protested Ella. "He said he lived at the Turret House. He doesn't. He showed me where Jock lived. That house is gone. The only other place I ever saw him was at school."

"What about the Royal?" asked Jesper. "You were with him there, Ella."

"Yes, I suppose," mused Ella. "He was friendly with Hong. But friendly enough to hide there? I don't think so."

"Well, it's something, at least," said Mr. Barclay. "Isbister, come with me. We must find him before he does any more harm."

Mr. Barclay turned on his heel and left the house. Ella desperately wanted to ask if Jock had survived his surgery but knew she could not. Could things get any worse?

Mrs. Barclay could not convince Ella to eat anything. She just dragged herself up the stairs, washed, and crawled into bed. She couldn't sleep. Her father's words were at war with her heart. She tossed and turned. She heard her father and Jesper come home. As quiet as a mouse, she opened her bedroom door and crept into the upstairs hall to eavesdrop.

"No, Alex, we didn't find him. Hong is in mourning for his lost friend, Ywe. Their customs are different from ours. The Royal is closed tight. He said the boy has not knocked on his door, and there is no place for him to sneak in. I believe Hong. We must keep looking."

Ella felt relief. Billy needed to be found, for his own sake. They had to get this matter cleared up. But not tonight. Her father was too angry. Tomorrow would be better. She had to find Billy and make him come and speak to her father. It was the only way. But where was he?

All night Ella tossed and turned. At dawn, she sat up straight in her bed. She knew where Billy was!

Quietly she eased out of bed and pulled on clothes. She inched out into the hall and down the stairs, trying to remember the location of each creaky board. At the door she chose her sturdiest boots, then gritted her teeth as she ever so carefully opened the door, just a crack, and squeezed through. She was out! She sat on the porch step to button her boots then raced across Victoria Park in the soft morning light.

Ella ran two blocks north along Cornwall Street, turning her eyes away from the wreck of the library as she passed. She still couldn't accept that her favourite spot was ruined. Just past 11th Avenue, she turned left and headed towards the Palace Livery.

In the quiet of the morning, all Ella could hear were the snorts and rustlings of the horses. Nobody was about. She checked the paddock. Horses, but no Billy. Cautiously, feeling a little nervous, Ella went into the stable. Half of it was crushed, so the horses were sharing stalls. In here, the air was close, warm and pungent. It smelled of sweet hay, acrid urine and leather polish. Ella looked into the first stall. The horses turned their big heads towards her but didn't approach the gate. Billy wasn't hiding there. She checked the next stall, and the next. The horses sensed her presence. They flicked their tails and whinnied. It made Ella nervous. But she had to find him. He had to be here.

In the next-to-last stall she saw him, asleep in the hay. She took two steps towards the gate, peering into the shadows while keeping a close eye on the horse inside the stall. Then she saw it was old Martha, and grinned. Martha was not so frightening. She went right up to the gate.

"Billy! Billy Forsythe! Wake up!"

Billy opened his eyes. When he recognized her, he jumped to his feet.

"Ella! What are you doing here?"

"You're in terrible trouble, Billy. I'm here to help you, but you have to tell me the truth. After the tornado, did you go to the bank and steal some of their money?"

Billy looked flabbergasted. "If I had stolen money, do you honestly think I would be sleeping here in a stable?"

"It's not the least bit funny, Billy. And if we're talking about honesty, you've got to start showing some. This is really serious. I believe you, but nobody else does. You have to come with me and explain to my father. If you don't, they won't ever look for the real thief and you'll get blamed for something you didn't do."

"Sounds like I'm going to get blamed no matter what," said Billy glumly. He sat back down on the hay. "If I turn myself in, they'll lock me up. And if they don't find the real thief, they'll keep me locked up. Maybe I should just run away."

"NO!" replied Ella. "That would be the worst thing you can do! You have to prove you're innocent or you'll be branded a thief for the rest of your life. Billy, I saw you out in the wheat field. You've got plans, I know you have. Don't wreck them!"

Billy said nothing. Ella waited patiently outside the gate. Finally Billy sighed. He stood up, nuzzled Martha then opened the gate.

"I'm done with running."

Together the two of them walked back to Ella's house. Neither of them said a single word more.

The house on Victoria Avenue was still quiet. Nobody was up. Ella led Billy into the kitchen and made him some breakfast. He was starving. He was on his third egg when Mr. and Mrs. Barclay came into the room. They stopped short. Jesper followed them. He looked shocked when he saw Billy.

"Mother, Daddy? I thought and thought all night, and this morning I thought of a place where Billy might be. So I went and fetched him. He wants to clear his name."

"Clear his name?" Jesper sneered. "That won't be easy."

"Quiet, Isbister," said Mr. Barclay. "Young man, I'll ask you once and I demand the truth. Are you or are you not a thief?"

Billy looked Mr. Barclay straight in the eye. "I have never stolen money, sir," he said. "But I stole a pair of trousers and a notebook. So, yes. I am a thief."

CHAPTER 13

A Splendid Optimism

Billy was taken to jail. Mr. Barclay said it was the safest place for him for the time being. Because as terrible as the theft was, it was nothing compared to the other trials the Queen City had to deal with that day. Billy would just have to wait. As he was taken away, Billy looked over his shoulder at Ella.

"Please check on Jock for me, will you?" he pleaded.

Ella couldn't promise anything.

Finding all the people was by far the most important task Regina faced. All that day and the next, Ella sat at the little desk in the Black Block and helped manage the lists. Three days after the tornado, every house and every building on Ella's map had an X across it. It had taken just three days for the energetic rescuers to account for every soul in the Queen City. All the injured were being cared for at various shelters set up around the city. The bereaved began to bury their dead. Beloved Scoutmaster George Appleby had an enormous funeral. Chief mourner at another, much smaller funeral, was a little white dog.

While scores of volunteers looked after the stricken residents of the city, others turned their minds to rebuilding. The task was enormous. So many buildings had been destroyed or damaged. But by the second day after the tornado, 700 carpenters were on the job. The city was paying the extravagant wage of sixty cents an hour and workers poured into the city. The work was approached systematically. First, teams of volunteers went through city streets, collecting and hauling away debris. Then fifteen teams of carpenters fanned out over the city. Some teams were responsible for fixing damaged homes so that families could move back in. Other teams concentrated on rebuilding homes that were destroyed. Still others started planning larger projects. And all the while more workers continued the new construction begun before the tornado struck. Regina simply did not stop. The city moved forward almost without missing a beat.

When Ella was no longer needed to put Xs on the map, she joined her father at the bank. Someone needed to sort all the letters pouring into the city with offers of help. Bank tellers opened the envelopes and collected the cash and cheques that were stuffed inside. Ella took the letters and sorted them, all the while wondering if Billy really had picked the lock of the petty cash drawer. How would he even have known money was kept there? Was he really an accomplished thief?

One pile of good wishes came from government officials around the world – letters from America, Japan, England, France and many other countries. Ella was amazed the news had spread so far and wide. And a very large stack of letters came from individuals, moved to contribute what they could to help the Queen City back on its feet. These were the letters Ella liked the best.

Someone in Australia sent $101.85. A Mrs. Weldon in Vegreville, Alberta, sent one dollar. A ten-year-old girl from Winnipeg emptied her piggy bank and sent eighty-six cents. His Royal Highness the Duke of Connaught sent $500.00 through his Equerry-in-Waiting. Ella wondered what an Equerry-in-Waiting was.

A beautifully handwritten note arrived. It said, "*Dear Sir. I feel sorry for your people especially the injured and those who were dependent on them that were killed. Accept this small contribution $5.00 it may in some way help to buy bread or clothing for some needy for a day. Sincerely, Chas. McCleary.*"

Ella was beginning to understand what charity really meant. It meant knowing what was needed, and organizing how to get it done. It was the IODE ladies sorting piles of clothes. It was the volunteers who shared their skills. It was the people who sent money. You could help a little or a lot, from far away or up close. You could help just one person if you wanted. Ella thought again of Billy. He was the one she wanted to help, if only she could.

Mr. Barclay collected Ella at the end of the day to walk her home. He looked exhausted. Everyone in the city was working so hard.

"Daddy, can we take one minute to collect my photos?" asked Ella.

"I suppose," he said wearily. Off they went to the pharmacy. Mr. Duncan looked harried.

"With all these sightseers in town come to look at the wreck of our city, I'm processing photos all day long!" he complained. "But I suppose it's worthwhile work, if it means that more will hear of our tragedy." Mr. Duncan looked through his drawer. "Here are your rolls, Ella."

Ella thanked him, and she and her father continued on their way home. Dinner was a quiet affair. Everyone was too tired to talk. After dinner, Mrs. Barclay went straight to bed. The others were not long to follow. Ella washed and changed into her nightgown, then flopped down on her stomach on her bed. Carefully she pulled the photographs from the first envelope and spread them out in front of her. Oh, her Brownie was a wonderful thing!

There was the picture of Hong. She remembered how serious he had looked when he first posed for the picture. Then Billy made him laugh. His clothes looked so exotic, and thinking of the food made Ella's mouth water all over again, even though she was full. It was a good memory, until she remembered the look on Hong's face as he gazed at Ywe's body.

The next photo was a little blurry. The man in the picture was moving, but he was recognizable. Jesper, trying to shake off Li's grasp and yelling at everybody. Ella looked at his face. Gone was his arrogant smile. His handsome face was contorted with anger, making it look mean and angry. It was not a nice picture.

There was the first photo she'd taken of the Ackerman Building, before the tornado, back when she'd felt like an explorer. Had it been only a week ago? She smiled sadly at the picture of Jock. It had been such a lovely day, and he'd made her laugh so hard her sides hurt. Now he was hurt, maybe dying.

Next was Billy in the wheat field, his smile open and happy. He looked almost joyful, if that wasn't a silly word to describe a very frustrating boy. It didn't say "thief" to Ella.

The last picture was one Billy had taken. It was sure and steady, so that even though the subject was a fair distance away, every detail was clear. The photo showed Jesper leaning against her father's Cadillac. It still seemed odd that he'd been given permission to take the automobile into the fields like that. Jesper had a cigarette in one hand. He was laughing. It looked like he was showing off. Five other young men were lolling about the Cadillac. They all had bottles in their hands and they all looked like Jesper: arrogant, superior and full of themselves.

Ella didn't like the look of any of them, although it was no longer a surprise to her that Jesper would have such friends.

Ella took the snapshots from the second envelope. The first picture on the roll was the one of her friends at the picnic. Wascana Lake was in the background, and all her girlfriends were lined up, arm in arm, up to their knees in the cool water. Everybody looked so happy. Behind them the photo showed the pergola and the boathouse, both gone now, obliterated by the ravaging wind. It was the last picture she'd taken before the tornado.

She wasn't sure she wanted to see the rest of the photos. Every picture told a story with an awful ending. One shot showed the mess that used to be Smith Street. Ella pulled out the photo she'd taken before the tornado and compared it with the second.

It made Ella want to cry.

The last picture was of her father's bank. It had suffered some damage, but not a lot. That was a good thing, because there was so much to do at the bank right now that they just couldn't afford to have it closed.

Ella wasn't sure exactly why she'd taken that photo. She'd been in such a rush to get to the Warehouse District that day. Compared to the other photos, it didn't show the tornado's fury. She looked more closely at the picture. There was something odd about it, something that wasn't right. But she couldn't figure out what it was.

Quietly, so as not to disturb the sleeping house, she tiptoed downstairs into her father's study and borrowed his magnifying glass. Back in her room, she examined the snapshot closely. There it was! Beside a broken window there was a shape that didn't belong. She peered at the shape. It was a man. A man holding a satchel under his arm, a man who looked furtively over his shoulder. A man who looked like a thief.

Ella gasped. She recognized that man. And it wasn't Billy.

CHAPTER 14

The Truth

Ella desperately wanted to wake her father and show him the picture. But he was exhausted and wouldn't want to listen. And it was too late to fetch Billy out of jail anyway. It would all have to wait until morning.

There was no point in trying to sleep. How could she not have guessed? All the pieces fit. She tossed and turned and finally her room began to lighten with the dawn. Morning at last.

Ella dressed neatly, then arranged the photos that she needed to show her parents and left them on her bed. She squirmed at the breakfast table, earning several black looks from her mother. Finally the meal was done.

"Daddy? Mother? May I speak to you privately in the study?"

"Ella, can't it wait? Isbister and I must be off to the bank to sort things out," replied her father.

"It will only take a moment," pleaded Ella. "It's important."

Mr. Barclay sighed and sent Jesper on to the bank alone. Mrs. Barclay looked mystified as Ella ran upstairs to get the photos. Once they were all settled in the study, she took a deep breath.

"Daddy, I have proof of who stole the money from the bank," she said bravely. "And I think it also tells us who stole the IODE money. But I have to start the story at the beginning. Will you listen?"

"Get on with it," Mr. Barclay said impatiently. "I know you don't want it to be Billy, but facts are facts, Ella."

"I know Daddy. Here's the first fact," she replied as she laid out the photo taken in the Royal Restaurant.

"I know I shouldn't have been at the restaurant. When I saw Mr. Isbister I was mostly worried that he would tell on me. Which he did," she added glumly. "It wasn't until after that I wondered what *he* was doing there. He was very angry at the Chinese men, and kept saying, 'I have to play! I have to play!' but they wouldn't let him. I didn't know what he meant, but Billy told me that men gamble in the basement. I think that Mr. Isbister wanted to gamble."

Mrs. Barclay caught her breath.

Ella laid the next picture on the desk. Mr. Barclay frowned. "What's my Cadillac doing in the field?"

"I wondered too, Daddy. Billy took this picture. It was the same day. He borrowed a buggy to take me to see the prairie, and coming home we spotted the car. It didn't make sense to me then. Jock told us that the other men were Remittance Men, and that they were rich and lazy."

"You rode in a buggy with Billy and this Jock? Alone?" gasped her mother.

"You promised you'd listen!" pleaded Ella. Mrs. Barclay frowned. Mr. Barclay was staring at the photo.

"This Jock of yours has a point about the Remittance Men,"

said Mr. Barclay. "I'm annoyed with Isbister. These photos show me that he likes to show off for his friends, and that he smokes and possibly gambles, but they don't prove he's a thief, Ella. He didn't have my permission to take the automobile, but I let him drive it so often he may have assumed the right. It's not that important."

Ella laid the third picture down on the desk. "I took this right after the tornado. I was on my way to the Warehouse District to find Billy. I didn't even see him then, not until the photograph was developed. It's like you said, Daddy. Photos can show you things you don't notice in real life."

"See who, Ella?" asked Mrs. Barclay. "I don't see anyone."

But Mr. Barclay did. He didn't even need the magnifying glass. "That scoundrel!" he shouted. "It was Isbister who accused the boy in the first place! Do you mean to tell me it was him all along?"

"The pieces fit, Daddy," said Ella quietly. "I want to show you one more photo."

"There's more?" asked Mr. Barclay in disbelief.

Ella laid the last snapshot on the desk. It was the one of Billy in the wheat field. "This is why I fought you so hard, Daddy. I didn't want to but I couldn't believe this boy," she said, pointing at the joyful picture of Billy in the wheat field, "could do the things you said. Please understand! I didn't mean to be disobedient, honest, I just had to...had to..." Ella wasn't quite sure how to say it.

"You had to fight for what you thought was right," said her mother gently. She looked thoughtfully at Ella. She didn't seem quite so angry any more.

Mr. Barclay wasn't thinking about Ella. Or Billy. He was seething with anger at Jesper. "I took that lad into my home, spent time with him, taught him. His father will be hearing from me, duke or no duke!" He stomped off to the bank. Jesper was going to get a surprise! Strangely, Ella didn't feel upset for him, just sad.

Then she turned to her mother. "What about Billy?" she asked. "What's going to happen to him?"

"One step at a time," replied her mother. "We still don't know who Billy really is, or where he belongs. I'll tell you what. Why don't we gather up some pens and notepaper and go to the Grey Nuns Hospital? I think it best you don't go to the bank today, so instead we could visit the wounded and offer to write letters to their families for them. Maybe it's time I met this Jock of yours."

Ella hugged her mother. "Oh yes, please!" she exclaimed. "You'll like him, Mother, he's very funny!"

The two of them set off towards the hospital. On the way, they stopped at the *Leader* office to pick up the day's newspaper. "Perhaps you can read it to some of the bedridden," Mrs. Barclay suggested. Ella nodded. She could do that.

The hospital was a bustling place. In truth, Ella had never been there before, never having needed broken bones to be set or gashes stitched up. Young ladies didn't engage in the sorts of activities that caused accidents, at least not usually. Not until a tornado blew the world apart. The waiting room was full of people, many bloody or nursing bashed arms or legs. There seemed to be dozens of doctors and nurses bustling about, small whirlwinds in themselves. As Mrs. Barclay talked to Miss

Clearihue at the desk about volunteering, Ella watched with interest as a white-capped nurse bent over a small girl with a nasty gash on her arm.

"You're a lucky girl, Laura. I'll be able to fix you up as good as new. But, my dear, can you be a brave soldier?" Ella watched as the little girl nodded her head uncertainly. "You see," went on the nurse, "it will hurt a little, I can't say that it won't. I want you to hold tight to your mommy, be brave, and right after we shall put a pretty bandage on your arm and get you ice cream. Can you do that?" The mention of ice cream made little Laura's eyes light up. Her nod was more certain this time.

As Ella watched, the little girl was rearranged on her mother's lap so that her hurt arm could rest on the table but her little face could be tucked into her mother's soft warm bosom. With loving arms tightly around her, Laura was indeed brave. And the few tears she had dried instantly when she was presented with her ice cream. Ella found herself grinning from ear to ear.

"Ella, this way!" called her mother. Clutching the newspaper, Ella and Mrs. Barclay made their way deeper into the hospital. Away from the waiting room, there was organized chaos. The wards were filled to bursting, with cots and stretchers in every corner. More stretchers lined the hallways. Family and friends clustered around loved ones. There were, to be sure, many in tears. Not all of the storm's victims could be saved. But the valiant doctors and nurses were doing all they could.

Ella's eye was caught by a young boy who looked to be tied down to his bed. "Hello," she said. "What's your name?"

"I'm Kenneth," replied the boy. "Kenneth Dunn. And I'm six years old."

"What a big boy you are!" laughed Ella. She looked curiously at all the straps tying him down. "It looks like you tried to escape, and the jailer has put you in a cage," she joked.

"I can't escape," the boy said glumly. "My leg's broke. And Nurse says I wiggle too much. So I got to be tied down. I don't like it much," he went on, wiggling like a little worm. "I want to get up!"

"Do you want me to tell you a funny story?" asked Ella.

Kenneth's eyes brightened. "Yes, please!"

Ella fought a tear as she retold Jock's story about the Gorbey. Would he ever tell another story? Make them laugh? Billy cared for the odd little man. Was Jock his father? If not, who was he? As usual, that brought Ella back to the beginning. Who, exactly, was Billy?

In spite of the questions filling her head, Ella left Kenneth laughing. In another bed, Ella recognized Amy James from school. Amy was only nine and in the junior class so Ella didn't know her well, but went to say hello anyway. Amy was happy to have someone visit.

"The wind blew our house right into the air!" she said in amazement. "My aunt and uncle were cut by the broken windows, but otherwise they're okay. I broke my collarbone. They're not here right now 'cause they have to find us a place to stay. Ella, I didn't know the wind could ever blow that hard!"

The next ward was filled with grown-ups. Some looked eagerly for company. Others were steeped in sadness, their heads turned to the wall. A nurse came up to Mrs. Barclay. "Can you speak to Mrs. Hodsman, please? She's badly hurt, but that isn't the problem. One of her little boys was killed and he's to be buried this afternoon. She hasn't even seen him yet. The poor dear! That's another of her boys in the cot beside her. He's only five and hurt as well, but such a little man. He's trying his best to cheer his mother but he could use some help."

"Of course I'll speak with her," replied Mrs. Barclay. "Ella, why don't you read the paper to that man with the bruised face?" Ella turned her head to the other side of the room. The wards were so crowded that men, women and children were all pushed together. Ella could see why her mother had noticed the man. He had been battered about the face and his eyes were swollen shut. Dark bruises reached down his neck, and covered the arms that lay on top of the coverlet. A little nervously, Ella approached the man.

"Would you like me to read you the morning paper, sir?" she asked.

"I'm that desperate for some news, young lady. I'd be much obliged," he replied politely. Glancing over at her mother, who had her arms around Mrs. Hodsman, Ella dragged a stool over to the man's bedside. She began.

"This is this morning's paper, July 3rd, 1912. Shall I read the headlines and you can choose?" The man nodded.

"Death list officially placed at 28. More than 300 wounded. An army of toilers clear debris in storm area; relief well organized. Banks will aid those in need, managers say. Financial men will place no obstacles in the way of customers. Civic relief fund is now over $50,000." Ella stopped. "My, that's a lot of money!" She went on. "There's a list of those who gave large sums of money. There's another list of people who are willing to share their homes with those who are homeless."

"Well, that won't be me," mumbled the man. "I haven't got a home any more."

Ella swallowed. "Mayor plans to rebuild destroyed section of city in one year. Long distance telephone connected both east and west, but local telephone calls months away."

"Why is that?" asked the man.

"It says they have located a new switchboard in Montreal, but that it might take several weeks to bring it to Regina. And a new telephone exchange must be built to house it. Would you like me to read you some more?" The man nodded.

"A rowboat was found jammed into a fourth floor fireplace in the Kerr Building, several blocks away from the lake."

"Ha!" snorted the man. "That must have given somebody a surprise."

Ella smiled. "Looting reported at Metropolitan Methodist Church."

"Read me that!"

"The robber was at work with a sledgehammer at the safe in the Methodist Church. Mr. Clarke, one of the trustees, happened to come at the most inopportune moment for the robber and scared him away. The safe at the time contained $260.00."

"My word," breathed the man. "Stealing from a church. Now, that's the lowest of the low!" Ella's heart went cold. It couldn't be Jesper again, could it? On top of everything else, was he a looter too? She felt sick to her stomach. But she tried not to think about it and read on until the man tired. Then she moved about the ward, writing letters or just chatting with those forced to stay abed. Some of the older women wanted nothing more than to hold her hand. They were so grateful for news and company that Ella felt almost guilty. She wasn't actually *doing* anything, but the patients seemed to think it was a great deal.

After a time, Mrs. Barclay tapped her on the shoulder. "We should go home for lunch," she said quietly. "The nurses need to feed everyone, and most will nap after lunch."

"May we see Jock before we go?" asked Ella.

"I've spoken with Matron about him. Yes, we may go, but Ella, Matron warns me that he is in very bad shape. Are you sure you want to see him?"

"I have to, Mother, so I can tell Billy," replied Ella. Mrs. Barclay nodded. They went deeper into the hospital where the most seriously ill were treated. A nurse pointed out Jock's ward. They tiptoed in.

He looked dreadful, unrecognizable. If the nurse hadn't said it was Jock, Ella would never have guessed. His thin, wiry frame, what she could see of it, was bloated and puffy from all the bruising and swelling. His head looked the size of a pumpkin. The rest of him was wrapped in bandages. Ella didn't want to imagine what lay beneath. Just then, Jock opened his eyes a slit. Was she imagining it, or was he trying to smile?

"Lassie," he whispered, then his eyes closed once more.

A tear rolled down Ella's cheek. Whatever was she going to tell Billy?

CHAPTER 15

Billy's Story

Mr. Barclay was already at home when Ella and her mother returned from the hospital. His face looked like a thundercloud.

"I trusted that boy! Clearly for no good reason other than the fact that his father is a duke, which is NO reason at all!" Mr. Barclay was shouting. Truly, the amount of shouting that had gone on in their quiet house this past week boggled Ella's mind.

"Did he confess?" asked Mrs. Barclay gently.

"He did. That boy is a coward! When confronted, he crumbled. Turns out his father stopped sending him an allowance. Told him he had a job and a place to stay – both thanks to ME! – so he should make good on his own. For all I know, I've been had! Maybe that duke knew all along his son was a wastrel. At any rate, Isbister couldn't keep up with his friends the Remittance Men, the ones still getting handouts from their daddies back in England, so he turned to gambling. When that didn't work, he became a thief. And it's not just your purse, Alex, or the bank. He even tried to rob the church!" Mr. Barclay put his head in his hands. That sick feeling was back in Ella's belly. Jesper was a gambler, a thief and now a looter as well. It couldn't get any worse. She wanted to cry for her father.

"The magistrate doesn't know what to do with him. It's the worst possible time for the city police to have to deal with one man's selfish behaviour. They are thinking of simply deporting him back to England. He's not the kind of man we want here to build Canada, after all. Let his father deal with him, I say!" Now Ella wanted to cry for Jesper. She remembered what he'd said that morning at breakfast, about how his father didn't want him. Could that be true? And if it was, what was Jesper trying to prove? He'd made everything much, much worse by being so foolish.

Ella and her mother ate in silence while Mr. Barclay simmered at the end of the table. Finally Ella could wait no longer. She had to ask.

"What about Billy, Daddy?" Mrs. Barclay looked sharply at her. *Now is not the time,* she seemed to signal. But Ella was worried. Billy had been in jail for two whole days already.

"Ah, yes, the wrongly accused. He's a problem, Ella, and again, one problem too many to have to deal with right now, with the tornado and all. No one quite knows what to do with him. He has admitted to breaking into the Regina Trading Company and stealing some clothes and a notebook. He will not say where he came from, or to whom he belongs. He may just have to stay in jail until the city has time to deal with him."

"That's not fair, Daddy! And he could help right now. He's a hard worker, and somebody has to look after Jock. Better he be out helping clean up after the tornado than locked up where somebody has to look after him."

"Where would he stay?"

"He could stay here."

"Absolutely not! We know nothing about him. Ella, he's just one person and there are so many right now who need attention. Why do you persist in helping *him?*"

"He's just one person, Daddy," replied Ella carefully, looking down at her plate, "but this is his whole life."

There was silence around the table. Finally Mrs. Barclay spoke. "She has a point, Leo."

Mr. Barclay looked at Mrs. Barclay across the table. He shook his head and sighed. "What are we to do with her?" he asked, in a somewhat bemused voice. When Ella heard it, she knew she had won. "Woe betide the man who must face a strong woman." He smiled wryly. "And now I have two of them!" Ella looked under her lashes at her mother. Alex, not Mrs. Barclay, looked back, and Ella could see the hint of a smile. All of a sudden, they were a team.

The Barclay family walked together to the magistrate after lunch.

"No, promises, Ella. He must tell us who he is before I decide if this will work. I'm not in a mood right now to extend the hospitality of my home to another thief!"

"Yes, Daddy," agreed Ella. That was fair.

Billy looked worried and upset when he joined the Barclays in the magistrate's office. He whispered to Ella urgently.

"How is he?" he asked under his breath.

"Still alive," she whispered back. Billy nodded his head and relaxed a bit. "Is it awful in jail?"

"I've lived worse. I'm sharin' with four blokes as got caught stealing a beer each 'cause they got hot when they was diggin' for bodies. Guess I'm a worse criminal than all of 'em!" The magistrate rapped his desk for silence.

"Young man," began the magistrate, "you have admitted to being a thief and a liar. Because of your behaviour, it was believed your crimes were numerous. Now that the true thief has been caught..." At this, Billy looked wide-eyed at Ella. She nodded slightly. "...your story becomes even more confusing. It is time to tell us who you are and where you came from, if we are to know what to do with you."

Billy sat up straight in his chair. "All right then. I'm ready." He took a deep breath. "Most of what I've said was true. I just didn't tell everything," he began. "I'm from Stepney, see, in London."

Mrs. Barclay made a small noise in the back of her throat. "I can tell, Missus, that you've heard of it. It's not the best place to live. Me mam, all she's got is seven boys and a drunken husband. Liked to drink all his pay at the pub. If she argued, he beat her. When I was about eight, I reckoned I was big enough to fight him back. So next time he went after me mam, I let 'im have it. 'Course he beat me up real bad. That was it for me mam. She took a frying pan to his head – that was a sight! Made him run and he never come back, so we was happy. Me, being the biggest, I went looking for work."

The magistrate interrupted. "You were eight years old then?"

"Yes, sir. Most folks didn't want me but I got real lucky. I was asking at the livery stables just when they was gettin' ready for a funeral. They needed a mute and said I'd do just fine."

Ella couldn't stop herself. "A mute? What's a mute?"

Billy smiled. "A mute jus' has to walk alongside the coffin in the funeral procession and look real sad. I kin look sad!" With that, Billy made his face look all pathetic. Ella laughed and even the magistrate smiled.

"They dressed me up in a black cape and a tall hat with black ribbons all down the back. All's I had to do was carry an ostrich feather and look miserable. And they paid me a shilling. A shilling! After that, they let me come round and do a bit of this and a bit of that and they paid me from time to time and everything was goin' good."

Billy's speech was slipping again. It made Ella smile.

"Me mam was crying one day when I got home. Crying from happy she said, but that didn't make no sense. She'd heard of this man Dr. Barnardo who was taking orphans and poor kids and sending 'em off to Canada for a new start. Me mam said she'd signed me up. I told her straight up I couldn't go 'cause who'd look after the boys, but she said I gotta. She said I had ta get outa Stepney. In Canada I could go to school, and I'd have enough to eat, and when I got all set I could send for me bruvvers and get 'em set up too. So it was decided. I was leaving.

"The boat was right fine," mused Billy. "Sometimes I wisht I never had to get off. We got fed real good, white bread at every meal. But then we got to Canada. Me, I got put on a train."

"I never imagined a place could be as big as Canada. The train kept goin' and goin,' night and day. Crikey! But after a long while the matron who was looking after us started putting kids off the train, one here, one there, with somebody waiting to pick 'em up. One morning it came my turn, but there weren't nobody there waitin.' Matron didn't like it, but the train whistle blew. She told me to wait right there, that somebody'd be along. Didn't know where I was, or where I was going. And nobody came."

Mr. Barclay and the magistrate frowned. Billy sighed. "Waited a long time. Nobody. Walked around a wee bit, but I was nowhere. There was nuthin' around, save the station and the grain elevator. The stationmaster didn't talk much. I remember I got to wondering what I'd do if nobody came. Would the stationmaster take me home? But late afternoon a brokedown buggy finally comes along. It was pulled by a couple of 'orses just as brokedown. 'Git up, boy!' says the man in the buggy, so I git. Didn't say another word. We rode in that buggy awhile and that man, he asked me how much farmin' I knew. I said, not much. And he said, 'So I thought. You're goin' to be trouble.' And I thought, I'm already trouble and I ain't even got there yet."

"It was dark and I was half starved by the time we got to his land. I hadn't et all day. But there weren't no dinner for me. He took me out to the barn and said 'Water the horses.' He never came back. I didn't know what to do after that so I slept in the barn."

Billy was silent for a bit. No one in the room said a word. "I learned to do everything on that farm. The disking, the ploughing, the seeding. I looked after them two brokedown 'orses, collected buffalo chips for the stove, hauled water, skinned rabbits, shovelled manure. I 'ad to, or he'd beat me. Come to that, he beat me anyway."

"One day the beatin' was real bad. Me brain was rattlin' in me head; I couldn't get it to quit. When my eyes stopped switchin' sides, I remembered what me mam said. She said, 'Whatever else 'appens, you got to go to school.' I weren't never going to school as long as I stayed with that man. I'd made a promise to stay, but he'd made a promise to treat me right. The deal was broke. So that night I up and left."

Mrs. Barclay gasped. Ella caught her breath. He was a runaway! Billy's face was tense. Mr. Barclay and the magistrate looked grim.

Billy looked Ella's father right in the eye. "That's when I became a thief. A carrot from one garden, a cabbage from another. A warm shirt off a clothesline. Never too much from one place, 'cause that weren't fair. I got real good at avoidin' dogs, I can tell you. Then after a time, I got to Regina."

"At first, I thought it'd be easier here, more like Stepney. Surely there'd be work for me. But I never got the tap. Until one morning. I felt a tap on me shoulder down at the hirin' hall. Work! But, no. It was Jock. He looks at me and says, 'You look hungry, boy. Come along with me.' And I did, 'cause I was. And he took me to the Royal and I et my first Chinese food. Then he took me home and I got a bath and I went to sleep in his bed. Think I slept for two days."

"Who is this Jock?" asked the magistrate.

"His name's Jock Ballogh," replied Billy. "He come from Glasgow to get his 160 acres, but didn't know what to do with it once he 'ad it. So the government took it away and give it ta somebody else. Jock came to Regina just like me, flat broke, 'ungry and looking for work. He got himself a job as night watchman at the Ackerman Warehouse and they let him live in the house next door, so he done okay. But he still had to find odd jobs to buy his food. He's no farmer, so he was finding it hard to get tapped. Like me.

"Once I woke up, Jock and me decided to work together. He'd share his roof if I'd get food for the both of us. And Jock helped with that. He knew the best jobs for boys like me, and he knew the blokes to talk to about it. I told him I was good with horses so he took me down to the Palace Livery. I could make a dollar here and there cleaning the stables and such. And Jock found out when the Settlers' Trains were arrivin' from America. Those Americans are well set; they bring lots of animals with 'em when they come. If I met the train, they'd give me a dollar to take care of the animals, give 'em water and stuff, while they was in town finding out where their land was."

Billy smiled a bit. "I found out you could buy ten meal tickets at the Royal for a dollar. That's a lot of eating for Jock and me!"

Ella smiled. She liked Hong's food too, but she wasn't sure she'd want to eat it every day.

"Things was going pretty good, working together like that. So after a time I told Jock what me mam said about school. And Jock, he says, 'You're a durn fool. Schools want to know all about ye. Ye go there, and they'll send ye back to the man.' But I promised me mam. I had to do it. Jock weren't happy, I can tell you."

"But he's a true friend as'll help you no matter what," Billy smiled a little. "So he says, 'If you must go, be careful.' Then I made up the story about Mr. Leatherby. I'd heard about him at the livery, see, and knew he never went out, so I thought it was pretty safe."

"And that's when you took my picture." He looked at Ella. "The only reason I got mad was 'cause I thought you'd show it to somebody and they'd send me back to the man. I was afraid. Then you told me to get better clothes so I broke into the store. I'm paying them back, though. I wrote down everything I took and twice now I've snuck a dime into the cash drawer when the shop lady wasn't looking. It's taking a while, though." Billy sighed as he looked down at his feet. "I really wanted boots, but I knew I'd never be able to pay 'em back."

Billy looked around at the others in the room. "And that's it. If you send me back to the man, I'll run away again, 'cause he'll kill me for sure. If you send me to jail, well, I've earned it, but I'll pay back the Trading Company faster if I can get out there and work. And I have to look after Jock," he stated firmly. "He's goin' ta need me."

Mr. Barclay looked at Billy thoughtfully. "Young man, do you know what you want to do when you grow up?"

Billy answered without hesitation. "Yes, sir, I do. On my eighteenth birthday I'm goin' to be at the Land Holdings Office before those clerks are even outa their beds. I'm goin' to sign up for my 160 acres and I'm not goin' to fail. I got four years till then to learn all that I can about farming and equipment and the best way to clear land. I need to know about adding and subtracting and how much it all costs. And once I'm set, I'm bringin' my bruvvers over. And when they're eighteen they're goin' to be waiting at the Land Holdings Office before the sun's up. And I'm goin' to make sure they bring me mam with 'em. She's gotta see this beautiful place she's sent me to."

There was silence in the room. Tears stood in Mrs. Barclay's eyes. Ella felt awed. Billy's determination humbled every last one of them. "You tell a remarkable story, young man," began the magistrate. Then he got up from behind the desk. "If you will excuse me for a moment, please." While they waited, a young woman brought cups of tea for everyone. In ten minutes the magistrate was back, and he had the owner of the Regina Trading Company with him.

The magistrate turned to the newcomer. "Mr. Lindeman, have you had any discrepancies in your cash drawers since the theft from your store?"

"What an odd question," replied Mr. Lindeman in a bemused fashion. "Twice now, we've had an extra dime in the cash register."

Well, thought Ella, if that wasn't proof, what was? She grinned at Billy.

CHAPTER 16

A New Start

"Don't fidget, dear," said Mrs. Barclay at breakfast.

Ella made a face. "But I'm so excited!" she complained. "I can't help it!"

Mrs. Alexandra Barclay smiled fondly at Ella. Only a week had passed since the storm, but things were getting back to normal. Every morning Ella awoke to the sound of hammers and saws. Teams of men moved methodically from the start of the tornado's path to the end, clearing rubble and making repairs. In one short week, one could almost be forgiven for not believing that a tornado had ever struck. In fact, the train-loads of gawkers that arrived daily often ended up disappointed with what they saw. "Made a big deal of nothing," they grumbled. "There's not much wrecked here." Their comments delighted Ella and her mother.

"Vultures!" stated Mrs. Barclay emphatically. "Nothing but vultures wanting to feed on the misfortunes of others. Serves them right if they don't get a free show. We've better things to do than pose for their entertainment!"

The subscription list was keeping Mr. Barclay very busy. He

still worried that there wouldn't be enough money to repair all the damaged buildings. Every day he met with government officials to ask for their help. Sometimes he came home smiling, but other times his face looked grim. Ella knew he'd find the money somehow. Her daddy wasn't going to leave anybody homeless. Including Billy.

Mr. Barclay wasn't the only Reginan hard at work. Mrs. Barclay and the ladies of the IODE were quick to remind the mayor and the councilmen that cleaning up the mess was only part of the job; that the thousands of homeless still needed clothes and pots and linens and dishes. And the donations kept pouring in. Ella sometimes thought that she'd never be finished sorting through the piles of clothes and toys and books, but she didn't mind one bit. Although it had only been two weeks since her first work party, it felt like she'd been part of the group forever.

Ella finished tying a big red bow around a square box. She was ready.

"Do you think he'll say yes?" asked Ella worriedly as she carried the box to the door.

"Don't get your hopes up, Ella," replied her mother. "The magistrate may have other plans for Billy. Stop fussing with your petticoat."

Ella frowned. Her cuts and bruises were getting itchy as they healed, but even so, the dreaded petticoat scratched her more. Some things never changed.

They collected Mr. Barclay at the bank and together the three of them retraced their steps to the magistrate's office. Mr. Barclay offered to carry the box but Ella didn't want to let it go.

When they arrived, Mrs. MacLachlan was waiting for them in the hall. Ella remembered her from the first work party.

"Thank you so much for coming," said Mrs. Barclay.

"Not at all," replied Mrs. MacLachlan. "This is important."

After a few minutes the four of them were ushered into the magistrate's office. "We're here about the boy," began Mr. Barclay.

"Billy Forsythe?" asked the magistrate.

"Yes. He and Jock Ballogh are both homeless. Mr. Ballogh will be out of hospital soon and will need a place to convalesce. Billy will want to be with him, and we have room for them both. There's no real need to keep him in jail any longer."

"Ah yes," said the magistrate. "I understand you have negotiated a payment plan between Mr. Forsythe and the Regina Trading Company?"

"Yes, he will sweep the floors every day after school until the debt is repaid. I have spoken with Mr. Ballogh and he's made it very clear he would like to become the boy's guardian. When he has fully recovered, I expect we will return to you to make that arrangement."

"I see no problem with that plan, Mr. Barclay. But are you certain you wish to take this on? I mean, with all your other responsibilities? Clearly he cannot go back to his Barnardo placement, but I'm sure we can find a foster home for him somewhere. Or we can send him home to Stepney."

No, no, no, thought Ella. *You can't!*

"True," said Mr. Barclay. "But my family seems to feel," at that Mr. Barclay smiled at his wife, "that the boy would be better off here. My daughter has taken pains to inform me that it is Mr. Forsythe's future, not his past, that is important. And after thoughtful consideration, I believe that she is right. Mr. Magistrate, this is a time for second chances. For the city and the boy."

Say yes, say yes!

"Well, Mr. Barclay, you are a man of impeccable character and if you feel this is a mission you wish to undertake I will not be the one to stand in your way. You are not the only person offering to take in strangers, and the city thanks you. I will send for my secretary to arrange the necessary documents."

Ella felt like jumping with joy. Only a frown from her mother stopped her from leaping up and cheering. The magistrate went on.

"Now about Mr. Isbister. We were able to recover the stolen money and return it to the bank, as you know. As for the earlier thefts, well, I'm afraid that money is already spent. The young man's deportation papers have been signed. Did you know that he is already on the train to Montreal? He will be shipped back to England from there."

"Yes, I know," replied Mr. Barclay.

Of course they knew. It was Mr. Barclay who had put poor Jesper on the train. It was Mr. Barclay who had given him stern advice to help him turn his life around. It was Mrs. Barclay who had hugged him for courage when he faced his father. And it was Ella who had helped Mrs. Dudek pack a lunch for the train. He'd made terrible mistakes, but he was still Jesper.

"Well then, I will have my secretary draw up the papers. If you will come this way, please?"

"One moment."

It was Mrs. Barclay. "What are you going to do about the

man who abused the boy?" she asked bluntly.

"What man?" asked the magistrate in confusion.

"The man who forced Billy Forsythe to run away to save his life," she said patiently. "The one who falsely accused the boy of stealing his life savings to trick the Mounted Police into looking for him. *That* man."

"Oh, yes, yes," the magistrate blustered. "I don't know that there is anything..."

"Mr. Magistrate," interrupted Mrs. MacLachlan as she stood and towered over him. "Since when has it been acceptable for children to be abused in their homes? I know for a fact that Dr. Barnardo wanted loving families for the children. This man betrayed the trust placed in him when he agreed to look after a boy. He must be punished."

Mrs. MacLachlan settled back into her seat and waited. Mrs. Barclay raised her eyebrows, questioningly. Ella held her breath. Mr. Barclay was smiling, just a bit, at the magistrate's discomfort.

"The man is apparently a homesteader. If he goes to jail, he will likely lose his land," argued the magistrate.

"Truly, I feel terrible for him," said Mrs. MacLachlan sarcastically. "We are part of a new nation. I'm sure you agree that we want upright men and women to build Canada."

"Of course," spluttered the magistrate.

"Fine," replied Mrs. Barclay. "You will let us know when he has been apprehended?"

"Of course," mumbled the magistrate. "I will contact the Mounted Police and have them investigate the matter."

"Good idea," agreed Mrs. Barclay warmly. "I do thank you for your help."

They all left the office. Ella was agog. Her mother was amazing. So was Mrs. MacLachlan. She couldn't wait to tell Billy what they'd done. Ella looked up at her mother with awe, in time to see her father brush her mother's hand. He leaned down and whispered, "Well done," in his wife's ear. Ella wasn't supposed to hear, but she did. She grinned.

"I'll stay to sign the papers," said Mr. Barclay. "Off you go, ladies, to collect your charge. Be quick, or Ella will be in a dither!"

It seemed to take hours before Billy was released from jail, but finally he was led into the waiting room. Ella jumped up.

"Billy!"

Billy's face was filled with amazement. "They tol' me, they said I was goin' to live with you?"

"That's right!" grinned Ella. "And Jock too, just until he's all healed up. Then the two of you can go wherever you want. Here, I've brought you a present."

Shaking his head in disbelief, Billy untied the bow. Inside were the very boots he had wanted so badly at the Regina Trading Company. The ones he couldn't afford to steal.

"Gad!" he exclaimed.

"Put them on!"

Billy put the boots on right there in the waiting room. "Best I ever 'ad!" he said in awe. It was only then that he noticed Mrs. Barclay and Mrs. MacLachlan. He instantly came to attention and smoothed down his hair.

"Good afternoon, Mrs. Barclay," he said, bowing. He turned to Mrs. MacLachlan. "Good afternoon, ma'am. My name is Billy Forsythe and I am pleased to make your acquaintance."

The ladies couldn't help but smile. "So you're the young man who stirred up all this fuss and confusion."

"No ma'am," replied Billy. "That was a cyclone."

Mrs. MacLachlan's eyes widened in shock, then she let out a guffaw of laughter. "I suppose it was, young man."

Laughing, the ladies linked arms. "Tea?" asked Alex.

"Absolutely," replied Ethel.

"Us too," said Ella. And they all four marched down Victoria Avenue towards home.

AUTHOR'S NOTE

The Regina Cyclone of 1912 was the deadliest tornado in Canadian history. Although Ella and her family come from my imagination, many of the people mentioned in this book experienced the tornado firsthand. Mayor McAra and City Commissioner Thornton are famous for the work they did to rebuild Regina. The Royal Northwest Mounted Police played a big role in the aftermath of the disaster, and today all members of the renamed Royal Canadian Mounted Police train in Regina.

Mr. Duncan, the pharmacist, was real, as was his wife Jennie. The experiences of Bruce Langton, Philip Steele and Leonard Marshall at Wascana Lake are true. The Hindson, Hodson and Beelby families, and most of the other tornado survivors who are mentioned in the book, are real, and Florence truly was rescued from inside a stove. The story of the little white dog is also true.

Although there was a would-be looter inside the church, it wasn't Jesper, who is a figment of my imagination.

To learn about the disaster, I looked at many photographs of the destruction and tried to imagine what it must have felt like to experience such a storm. I read books about the event, consulted city records, and looked at many of the letters sent by officials. And I read old copies of the *Leader* newspaper to find out what people were saying back in 1912. For more information about historical sources, as well as some very funny items I found in the newspaper, please check out my website at www.pennydraper.ca.

Tornado or Cyclone?

When Mayor McAra wrote thank you letters to donors after the disaster, sometimes he referred to the storm as a cyclone and other times as a tornado. So which is it?

A cyclone usually refers to a rotating mass of air. The air rotates counter-clockwise in the northern hemisphere and clockwise below the equator. It often brings rain or snow but is not necessarily dangerous and doesn't touch the ground. A tornado is spawned from that same rotating mass of air, but includes a dangerous column of spinning air that reaches down from the cloud and touches the ground. A tornado is smaller than a cyclone, but deadlier. So Regina's storm of 1912 is officially a tornado, but is usually known as "The Regina Cyclone." Tornados are rated on the Fujita Scale, which gives each storm a number between 0 and 5. In this scale, 5 is the worst, a killer storm. The Regina Cyclone is officially rated F4, because it is thought that wind speeds reached 400 kilometres per hour. But it was impossible to measure wind speed accurately in 1912. Some reports suggest that the funnel actually spun at 800 kilometres an hour and if that is true, then it was really an F5. Whatever the number, it remains the deadliest tornado in Canadian history.

Storm Stats

More than 2,500 people were left homeless by the storm. Five hundred buildings were destroyed. Property damage has been estimated at $1.2 million, which is about $24 million today. To help raise the money, the homeless were charged 25 cents a night for a cot in the park, and homeowners were charged for the removal of rubble from their homes. Even so, it took 46 years for Regina to pay off the debt.

Women

The early 1900s was an exciting time on the Prairies. Opening the west meant that everybody had to work. All of a sudden women were allowed to do things – had to do things – they had never done before.

Some women tried jobs that used to be reserved for men. In 1912, Alberta's Tillie Baldwin became one of the first female rodeo riders, for example. (Tillie could ride two horses at once, standing with one foot on each horse – cool!) But most women preferred to stay at home doing volunteer work. They formed groups like the Imperial Order of the Daughters of the Empire and the Women's Canadian Club. The groups offered companionship, advice and laughter. But that's not all that went on at their meetings. Quietly working in the background, women like Alexandra Barclay became very powerful.

Men could clear the land and grow the wheat, but those tasks alone did not bring fulfillment. The women concerned themselves with building a well-rounded society, one that was not only successful but happy. They looked after culture, music and literature. They organized schools and hospitals. Ensuring that every child had a book to read was a high priority. And as they did volunteer work in these areas, they saw problems the men were missing – problems like Billy. To do something about those problems meant they needed even more power. So they decided to change history. They asked for the right to vote, just like the men.

Two of the women mentioned in this book were real. Nellie McClung is one of the most famous women in Canadian history. She lived in Manitoba, and it was largely due to her that women in Manitoba were the first in Canada to win the right to vote in 1916. Nellie McClung was also a member of the Famous Five, a group of women who asked the Government to recognize women as "persons." They won their petition. As a woman living today, it's hard for me to imagine what it would feel like not to be considered a "person".

Nellie did write the play mentioned at the work party in the book, although she actually wrote it in 1914, not 1912. It was such a funny story I had to include it, even if that meant changing the date a little. I hope nobody minds.

Ethel MacLachlan, who insists the man who beat Billy be punished, is also real. She was a teacher for many years before moving to Regina in 1909. There she became a secretary in Saskatchewan's Department of Neglected Children. In no time she was much more than a secretary. She firmly believed that all children had the right to a happy childhood and worked hard to ensure no child was neglected. In 1917 Ethel became the first female judge in the province, presiding over the newly-created Juvenile Court where she continued to help kids like Billy.

The Kodak Brownie Camera

While doing the research for this book, I found many, many photographs. The pictures in this book are real archival photos taken in Regina directly after the disaster. Because there were more photos, in fact, than written reports, I decided to make Ella a photographer and imagine that she had taken the photographs. It became an interesting way to use the historical materials as part of the story.

The Kodak "Brownie" camera, launched in 1900, was perfect for her because it was so easy to use. Back then there was even a Brownie Camera Club, where kids could enter contests and win prizes for their photos. It was, in fact, designed and marketed for children and that's why it was called a Brownie.

The Brownie was a cartoon character created in 1900 by a man named Palmer Cox and the character was as popular as Mickey Mouse is today. Cox's Brownie was used to help sell many different products besides the camera including dolls, games, trading cards and even cigars and ice cream!

A famous photographer named Ansel Adams started his career with a Brownie camera. In 1916, when he would have been about the same age as Ella, he was given his first Brownie. One day Ansel was taking a picture of a famous mountain called Half Dome when he slipped off a cliff. While tumbling down, he clicked the shutter. When his film was developed, the owner of the photography shop came to talk to him. "How did you get such a perfect picture – upside down?" Adams had to own up that it was an accident. As it turned out, the picture that later made him famous was another picture of Half Dome, and that one was no accident.

Believe It or Not

The cyclone really did reach into the Department of Education Offices in the Legislature and blow all the provincial examination papers away. Senior students like Ella who had written Provincial Exams during the week previous lost all their marks. Teachers had to go back to their notes and assign each student a new mark based on their class work over the year.

Another famous disaster occurred in 1912. Three months before the cyclone, the mighty Titanic sank. Mr. and Mrs. Blenkhorn from England had tickets for the great boat's maiden voyage. However, they were married just before the boat was due to sail and their wedding party was such fun that they were late to the dock. They missed the boat. Taking a later sailing on another boat, they only learned the fate of the Titanic when they arrived in Canada. It appeared the party had saved their lives.

The Blenkhorns went on to make their home in Regina and happened to be walking across Victoria Park just as the cyclone hit. Caught out in the open, the Blenkhorns were snatched away by the wind. Neither one survived. They had come 8,000 miles to meet their fate.

A man named William Pratt was appearing in a play in Regina at the time of the tornado. Pratt volunteered as a rescue worker, and he and the other actors put on benefit concerts to raise money for rebuilding. Years later, Pratt moved to Hollywood, changed his name, and became famous for playing the role of Frankenstein and providing the original voice of the Grinch in *How the Grinch Stole Christmas*. His new name? Boris Karloff.

In Memoriam

Scoutmaster George Appleby: emigrated from England three years earlier

Frank and Bertha Blenkhorn: born in England

Andrew Boyd: retired farmer

Ywe Boyuen: worker at Mack Lee's Chinese Laundry

Joseph J. Bryan: age 51, manager of Tudhope-Anderson

James Patrick Coffee: born in Lisbon, Ireland

George B. Craven: age 35, born in New Zealand, dairy instructor

Arthur Donaldson: contractor, owner of a small white dog

Robert Fenwick: killed in Mulligan's barn

Miss Etta Guthrie: seamstress, engaged to be married

Mrs. R. W. F. Harris: wife of accountant R. W. F. Harris

Fred Hindson: medical student, brother of Douglas Hindson

Lawrence R. Hodsman: son of James R. Hodsman

Donald Miller Loggie: infant child of Mr. and Mrs. H. N. Loggie

Laura McDonald: killed while trying to close the chicken coop

James McDougall: machinist for Cockshutt Plow Co. and his daughter Ida, age 3

Mrs. Paul McElmoyle: grocer's wife, mother of three small children

Isabelle McKay: maid at a local hotel and her son Charles, age 3

Andrew Roy: visiting from Horwick, Quebec

Charlie Sand (Yenason): worker at the Mah Chang Sing Laundry

James Milton Scott: clerk in the Customs Department

Mary Shaw: born at Elgin, Ontario, wife of Samuel, CPR yardman

Vincent H. Smith: real estate agent

Philip Arthur Richard Steele: age 11

Ye Wing: worker at the Mah Chang Sing Laundry

From the Regina Leader, July 3, 1912

ACKNOWLEDGEMENTS

A big thank you goes to the staff of Coteau Books who shared their home city with me as we worked together on this project. Your comments, impressions and memories of cyclone stories truly helped shape this book. Working with such a great team has been a truly rewarding experience.

I would like to thank Dana Turgeon, Historical Information and Preservation Supervisor, Office of the City Clerk in Regina for her assistance in locating pictures and materials and for offering a wonderful space for me to work as I completed my research. Thanks also to the staff at the Dr. John Archer Library, University of Regina, for teaching me how to use their jazzy microfiche machines.

I would also like to thank the Hayward clan of New Zealand for allowing my characters to use their names. I've only borrowed the names – please remember that the personalities are completely fictional!

A big box of chocolates is reserved for my staff and colleagues at the University of Victoria, without whom I could not have balanced work and play.

Once again, it has been the greatest of pleasures to work with my editor, Barbara Sapergia. I so enjoy our talks and your viewpoint.

And I always save the best for last. Thank you, Dale. Without you none of this would be possible.

ABOUT THE AUTHOR

PENNY DRAPER is an author, a bookseller and a storyteller who lives in Victoria, BC. Originally from Toronto, she received a degree in Literature from Trinity College, University of Toronto, and attended the Storytellers' School of Toronto. For many years, Penny shared tales as a professional storyteller at schools, libraries, conferences, festivals and on radio and television. She has told stories in an Arabian harem and from inside a bear's belly – but that is a story in itself.

Penny's books have been nominated for numerous awards in Canada and the United States. They have been honoured with the Victoria Book Prize, the Moonbeam Award Gold Medal and the Chocolate Lily Readers' Choice Award (runner-up). *Day of the Cyclone* is part of Coteau Books for Kids' *Disaster Strikes!* series. The series also includes Penny's *Terror at Turtle Mountain*, *Peril at Pier Nine*, *Graveyard of the Sea*, *A Terrible Roar of Water* and *Ice Storm*.